THE WHISPERING

THE WHISPERING

CHARLOTTE J. RUTH

For Jocelyn, without whom this story would be very different.

Prologue

At first glance, one would have confidently declared that Winter Barnes was an introvert. Preferring to work alone in a group project, linger in her room, or lose herself in countless works of literature rather than riding bikes and annoying the neighbors appeared to be inherently introverted qualities. It's important to note that Winter used to have a best friend. In the seventh grade, she'd been particularly close with Adam Williams. The two were inseparable: a rather elaborate secret handshake that their classmates failed time and time again to figure out, visiting the infamous Roseberg Diner with regularity, and frequently dwelling in the abandoned movie theater were some of the many unusual activities they took part in together.

To the great chagrin and sheer disappointment of many individuals unwilling to accept or admit to the blunt truth, not all friendships last forever. On the eve of the first night of Redwick's traveling summer carnival, Adam was snatched away from his own home. Kidnapped. His family never did quite manage to find him, nor did they know the identity of the kidnapper. Two weeks after his disappearance, the police declared him to be dead, despite his body remaining unfound. The case remains an infamous Redwick mystery, the story shoved away in the dusty, old newsroom of the Town Hall, forgotten by most once a new story came along. But Winter never forgot.

Before she knew it, it was September, the start of her seventh-grade year, and everyone else seemed to have moved on from Adam's disappearance. He was mentioned once in a while, referred to by her classmates as "that nice but weird kid who died" or "that poor, innocent

1

young boy," as referred to by adults, remarking that he was "taken from us so soon. The poor thing. May he rest in peace." Winter refused to accept any of it. They'd never even found his body; why should he be presumed dead? She knew he was still out there. One way or another, she was going to see him again. One day... right?

As the school year came and went, Adam became history. It had been one year since his disappearance and he still hadn't been found. Her belief that he would eventually be found dwindled as she realized that the likelihood of him being dead rather than alive seemed more and more possible as the days went on. She had almost lost any hope that he would come back. That all changed on the eve of her thirteenth birthday.

Chapter One

Let us now pause for a brief introduction to the town Winter resides in. We will forget about her troubles for a moment, basking in the innocence that was *before*. Ignorance is bliss, as they say.

Redwick is a quiet town, situated near the forest in upstate Washington. Small shops inhabit the streets, varying from vintage record stores to second-hand clothes shops. That being said, Redwick is most prominently known among travelers for its main street, Woodridge Lane. Woodridge contained all sorts of shops, from old-timey diners to kitschy antique stores to warm and inviting coffee shops. Pedestrians linger by shops, catching up with friends, while others sit on wooden benches, escaping into another world through a book. A town favorite is the Roseberg family diner and ice cream shop, cleverly named "Roseberg's." A rather large chalkboard out front contains warm and welcoming messages that various employees rewrite daily, such as, "Come into Roseberg's, where you'll always find a pal to keep you company." Adam and Winter were two of the shop's most regular customers, the most frequent customer being Mr. Charleston, a friendly, kind old man who lived just down the street from Winter herself. Adam ordered strawberry ice cream every time without fail. Winter preferred more exotic flavors, namely peppermint chocolate chip.

Winter's personal favorite place on Woodridge was the old movie theater. While it was run-down, it wasn't completely closed. There were cover band shows, school theatrical performances, and sometimes even movie showings there. However, it tended to be empty. It was a place of comfort for her; a place to go when she couldn't handle the real world.

She liked to imagine what the theater was like when it first opened, losing herself in the idea of the smell of freshly popped popcorn, the feel of the brand-new leather seats, and the sound of an old movie playing while the viewers theorize about what might happen next.

For Winter, the present was boring; a constant that lacked excitement or adventure. She always knew what she would do and what everything would look like, sound like, or even smell like, day after day. The only anomaly was Adam, a constant source of bright, playful energy that could never bore her even on the dreariest of days. Rather than living in the present, like her parents told her to, or in the future, like her teachers told her to, she preferred the past. The past was unknown; a world that most currently living souls could not remember. To her and Adam's luck, Redwick was home to an abandoned movie theater full of preserved history and hidden gems of excitement. The two of them frequently escaped the predictability of their lives by journeying to the past for an afternoon at a time. Winter craved adventure, but Redwick's predictability disagreed with her.

Chapter Two

Winter opened her eyes, blocking out the morning sun with her fingertips. Something about today felt different, she thought. She pondered this as she opened her window, letting in the fresh August air.

She laid back in bed for a moment, absorbing the peacefulness of the morning. It was her favorite time of day simply because of how quiet the world was. If she wanted to go on an adventure without being bothered by anyone, she could.

The warm, comforting aroma of pancakes cooking in the pan and hot chocolate being brewed on the stovetop, just for her, jolted her out of her peaceful trance.

Pancakes and homemade hot chocolate could only mean one thing -- it was her birthday.

Footsteps sounded their way across the second floor. They were clean but heavy, meaning they belonged to her dad. She jumped out of bed, ready to greet him.

He knocked on her door. "Knock knock?"

"Who's there?"

"Hoo."

"Hoo who?"

"Are you an owl?"

Winter laughed as her dad flung her bedroom door wide open, his arms wide as he brought her in for a suffocating yet sweet hug. "Hey, kiddo. Haven't seen you since you were twelve!"

Winter rolled her eyes playfully. "Dad... come on. That's the most overused dad joke of all time. I know you can do better than that."

He mock-gasped, pretending to look offended. "I can't believe you just said that. It's the *second* most overused dad joke of all time. The most is 'I haven't seen you since last year!' Come on, Winter. Get your dad jokes straight."

She chuckled. Her dad broke into a grin, the corners of his deep brown skin uplifting into a sweet smile. He pulled her in for another hug. "Happy birthday, my little teenager."

Just then, another set of footsteps echoed their way towards her room. In contrast to her dad's, they were light but precise, meaning they belonged to her mom.

Her mom walked through the door, a smile beaming on her pale but comfortingly warm face as she gave Winter a hug not nearly as suffocating as her dad's. "Happy birthday, sweetie."

"Thank you!" She paused, a sly grin creeping across her face. "Is that hot chocolate and pancakes I smell?"

"It sure is," her dad answered.

"Well, what are we waiting for? Those pancakes won't eat themselves!"

* * *

The Barnes family sat at the kitchen table, relishing the scrumptious breakfast they had just consumed.

"I'm surprised you're being this patient," her mom began. "Your presents are sitting just over there!" She pointed to the fireplace, where Winter's birthday gifts lay.

"Oh, yeah. I'll open them later. Thank you, though." She stood up, pushing her chair in.

"Hey, where are you off to?" her dad asked. "Last year you could hardly finish your breakfast before you rushed over to open your presents."

"I'm just going to my room."

Her parents exchanged nervous glances. Winter knew where this was going, where it always went.

"Winter..."

"Mom, I'm fine. Stop worrying about me, please."

Her mom's gaze softened. "We know you've been wanting to spend more time alone since-"

"Since Adam disappeared?"

Her parents froze.

"Honey, he didn't just dis-"

"I know what I said," Winter shouted. "He's. Not. Dead."

"Winter, even if he were alive, they would have found him by now," her dad said.

"No, you're just saying that because you've given up hope like everyone else has."

"That's not what I meant, and you know it," he said firmly. When Winter froze, overtaken with guilt, he relaxed. "Look, kiddo, we just want you to be happy. There's nothing you can do about Adam. It's a terrible situation, and you shouldn't have to be going through this. Grief is a long process. It takes time. It's true that he was never found, but the search was abandoned. Even if he is still out there, every day that goes by decreases the likelihood that that scenario is possible. Either way, he's gone. The best you can do is to remember him and make some new friends."

"Look, I know I haven't been the best daughter. I go up to my room and shut you guys out. But can't you let me have this just for once? It's my birthday, for God's sake. I want to be with the only person in this house who believes me: myself." With that, she stomped upstairs.

* * *

Winter shut her door, blocking out the concerned shouting of her parents. This had gone on for far too long. "Why... can't... they... just... be... normal!" she shouted through gritted teeth.

Winter glanced around her room, her bed catching her eye. Its comfort welcomed her as she carelessly flopped onto it, breaking the surface tension. She sat there for a while, reflecting upon the argument.

We know you've been wanting to spend more time alone

We just want you to be happy

The best you can do is to remember him and make some new friends
Make some new friends.

It was too much. Tears streamed down her face. She tried to blink them away, but the force of her salty tears was stronger than her desire to conceal her emotions.

It's your birthday, she thought. *You're not supposed to be crying.*

Winter rarely cried. The fact that the one time she was crying ended up being on her birthday struck her as ironic. She began to laugh, wiping away the tears.

"Okay," she said out loud. "Get a hold of yourself."

Deciding that distracting herself was probably the best idea, she went to look out the window to observe. One of her favorite activities was watching passersby walk by her house and go about their days. It wasn't stalking; she was just curious. Everyone lived separate lives, and despite the fact that she probably would never talk to anyone she watched, she was fascinated by the idea of witnessing a small part of their day.

The person of interest today was a short, stout man walking his dog. Winter wasn't sure what breed the dog was, but it looked like some type of terrier. The man was walking his dog while licking the ice cream on the cone in his hand. Winter squinted to interpret the flavor. It looked pink, like it could be strawberry-flavored.

Strawberry, Winter thought. *Adam's favorite ice cream flavor.*

She sighed, feeling the oncoming rush of tears. *There's no use in crying now,* she thought, rapidly blinking to force the tears away. A single tear dripped down her face, but before a second could succeed it, she was struck with an idea.

You know what might make you feel better? Ice cream! she thought as she hastily threw on the first clothes she could find in her closet -- her "Pizza Planet" t-shirt, a worn-down pair of blue jean shorts, and some socks -- and her Hello Kitty backpack (you could *never* be too old for these things).

With a sudden air of positivity, Winter flew downstairs.

"Going somewhere?" her mother asked nervously.

"Yep! Gonna get some ice cream."

Winter didn't check to see the concerned glance between her parents, but she knew it was there.

"Be careful, okay?"

"Okay."

"Be back by six! You don't wanna miss your pizza and movie marathon!" her dad informed, referring to her annual birthday tradition of ordering pizza and rewatching her favorite movies (Tim Burton's rendition of *Alice in Wonderland*, *E.T.*, and *Coraline*).

"I wouldn't miss it!" she responded, sprinting out the door.

Chapter Three

Winter flew down the street, nearly dropping her backpack. The blazing August sun shined down on her shoulders, causing her to sweat. She didn't care about the sweat, though. There were more important matters at hand. She kept on running.

Finally, she thought, panting, skidding to a halt in front of Roseberg's. She walked into the welcoming air-conditioned diner, appreciating the cool air against her forehead.

The diner-slash-ice cream shop was cute and quaint like the rest of the shops in Redwick, but Winter believed this one to possess its own unique charm. There was an old bell that rang whenever a customer entered the diner, pairing nicely with the vintage checkered floor. There were booths and small, round tables, one of which Mr. Charleston sat at. Winter felt bad for him. He was approaching ninety, which Winter thought would be a milestone to celebrate, but everyone knew his birthdays were anything but celebratory ever since his brother's disappearance. His brother, Richard, was last seen on Mr. Charleston's fifteenth birthday; ever since his mysterious disappearance, Mr. Charleston hadn't been the same. He sat in the back corner of the diner, reading a crinkly newspaper, his head tilted down.

There were three menus upon the wall: the drinks menu, the breakfast menu, and the lunch/dinner menu. Winter had no interest in getting a meal that day, so she walked over to the ice cream bar. Roseberg's prided themselves on their wide variety of flavors. They had thirty-six, ranging from classic vanilla to rainbow cake batter.

"Heya, Winter!" shouted the owner of the diner, Mrs. Roseberg. "Happy birthday! It's on the house today."

"Oh, thank you, but-"

"Nonsense. Anything for our favorite customer." She glanced at Mr. Charleston, whose gaze had shifted to Mrs. Roseberg's in speculation. "Our *other* favorite customer. You know you're both the favorites, right?"

"Sure, sure. No need to make excuses. I'm just a grumpy old man, right?"

Mrs. Roseberg's eyes narrowed. "You'd be incredibly naive to believe that I think that of you. In fact, I think just the opposite. You're a stubborn, cunning, strong-willed man." Her eyes widened in dramatic effect, then softened. "But you're still one of my favorite customers."

Mr. Charleston chuckled. "You've barely changed."

"Neither have you."

Mrs. Roseberg turned abruptly to face Winter, as if she'd forgotten she was there. "I'm sorry, honey. Us older folks tend to get carried away sometimes. What can I get ya?"

"Hmm. I'll have..."

"Take your time," she said. "I'll be here all day."

She browsed the array of flavors, her gaze shifting from the cake batter to the chocolate chip cookie dough to her beloved peppermint chocolate chip. She wanted to try something different, something she wouldn't usually get.

Get a scoop of strawberry, a faint voice hissed in her ear.

She looked around, but the diner's other two occupants were silent. *What was that?* Had she imagined it?

She shook her head of any unwanted thoughts. "Could I have two scoops of peppermint chocolate chip in a waffle cone?"

One scoop of peppermint chocolate chip. One scoop of strawberry.

She widened her eyes.

"Dear, is something wrong?" Mrs. Roseberg inquired.

"Uh, no, I'm just-"

Your favorite is peppermint chocolate chip. Adam's is strawberry. It's like you're together again. What more could you ask for?

Winter jolted.

"Are you sure you're alright?" Mrs. Roseberg asked, serious concern flitting across her face.

"Yeah, I'm fine. Could I change my order? One scoop of peppermint chocolate chip, one scoop of strawberry."

Mrs. Roseberg wasn't convinced, but she knew better than to bring up Adam. She was one of Winter's only confidantes who didn't judge her for believing Adam was still alive. As for whether she herself believed him to be out there, Winter didn't know.

"I recommend the chocolate crunch cone with that. It goes nicely with the peppermint and with the strawberry. There's no better combination if you ask me."

"Alright, chocolate crunch it is!"

Winter dropped a hefty tip into the tip jar, the drop of the coins echoing around the glass, the crisp bills silently falling to the bottom.

"Oh, sweetie," Mrs. Roseberg began, but Winter insisted. She gave Winter an approving nod. "That's very kind of you. You're shaping up to be a fine young lady. Just what this world needs."

"Thank you, Mrs. Roseberg"

"Sweetie, we've been over this. Call me Minnie."

Winter felt guilty calling an adult by their first name. She'd been taught it was rude. Just this once, she figured. "Okay. Thank you, Minnie."

Mrs. Roseberg -- Minnie -- nodded in acceptance. "That will do. Have a lovely birthday."

As she waltzed her way over to the exit, she noticed Mr. Charleston. She wondered if they were alike. Did anyone ever sit with him? Was he lonely like her, because of a loved one's disappearance?

"Hello?" Winter squeaked timidly. She swallowed in embarrassment.

Mr. Charleston looked up over his paper, not bothering to put it down. "May I help you?" his raspy voice answered.

Winter froze, unsure how to connect with him. "I was just wondering... could I maybe... talk to you about your brother?"

Mr. Charleston sighed. "Normally, I'd say no. But you aren't just a normal girl." He gestured for her to sit at his table. "What would you like to know?"

"What happened on the day he disappeared?"

Mr. Charleston slumped deeper into his chair, casting his gaze downwards. Winter felt bad for bringing up something that clearly upset him to talk about. "It was my fifteenth birthday, August thirteenth. It was the last day of the traveling summer carnival, so Richie and I decided to go."

Winter's eyes widened. "The carnival was open back then?"

Mr. Charleston let out a hefty laugh. "Yes. I'm not ancient, you know. The carnival has been around since the 1880s. Anyways, when we'd arrived at the carnival, Richie wanted to play games, but I told him I was 'too old' for games and that I shouldn't have brought him here. He got upset, saying he was going to go explore some attraction or other, I don't remember what. So, I abandoned him to go play with my friends." His gaze shifted to the ground. "How I wish I'd never done that. It's my biggest regret."

"That's silly. You couldn't have known," Winter consoled him.

He nodded. "That may be true, but that doesn't mean I don't blame myself. Before I knew it, the police had arrived to search the scene for Richie. He was never found. He was presumed dead. But I believe he was still out there, living a better life, having no desire to come back to a town that had lost hope." He shook his head. "You must think I'm crazy."

"What? No! I believe you, really. I think the same thing happened to Adam, actually. He disappeared at the carnival, too." She paused. "You probably think *I'm* crazy."

"No, I don't. I believe you."

Winter gasped. "Really?"

He nodded, continuing. "When last year's events transpired, the circumstances were too similar to Richie's disappearance to be a coincidence. I knew they had to be related." He looked Winter in the eye. "I've spent decades of my life pondering 'what if,' and it's not getting me anywhere. I'm sorry, Winter. There's nothing more I can do. I'm growing old, and I'd like to spend my remaining time being with the people I love. I suggest you do the same."

Winter stood up aggressively. "What? That's it? You just gave up and lost all hope?"

"Everything alright over there?" Mrs. Roseberg asked, shooting a concerned look over at the two.

"Yes, Minnie, we're quite alright," Mr. Charleston responded. He turned back to Winter. "Let's step outside."

"Bye, Minnie! Thank you for the free ice cream!"

"Oh, of course, dear. Thank you for the tip. Have a wonderful birthday!" She waved goodbye.

Winter followed Mr. Charleston outside. They found a small table outside the diner and sat down, facing each other.

Mr. Charleston sat up. "I'm not saying I've lost hope. I firmly believe that this unusual kind of disappearance is not circumstantial. It has happened too many times to be a coincidence." He paused. "There was another victim."

Winter's eyes opened wide. "What do you mean?"

"Her name was Amelia Sunbury. Well-mannered, bright, and sweet." He scoffed. "Always told you when you were wrong. She was a stubborn one, but she stood up for what she believed in. She would've made a name for herself, I'll tell you that." He sighed. "But, as these things go, she disappeared at the summer carnival in August of '57. No one knows why these three disappearances were so similar. They were marked as coincidences, but I believe otherwise."

"If you believe in it, why aren't you doing anything to stop it?" Winter asked, realizing too late how rude she'd sounded. "I'm sorry, I didn't mean it like that."

"It's alright," Mr. Charleston said, putting up a hand to stop her. "Don't think I haven't tried. I used to spend hours at the library archives, scavenging for anything related to the day Richie disappeared.

I spent so much of my youth fixating on my brother's disappearance that I lost my friends at school. They claimed I was too involved in the case and that my 'childish obsession' with finding him needed to stop. I refused to let go, of course, so they left me alone, leaving me in the past."

"What? That's terrible!" Winter shouted, indignant. "They couldn't have been your real friends if they just left you like that. You didn't deserve to be treated like that."

Mr. Charleston lightened. "That's what I like about you, Winter. You're loyal. You understand the true values of friendship. Not many people do these days, I'll tell you that."

Winter looked down at her shoes, ashamed. "No, I'm not a good friend. If I was, I would've found Adam by now."

"Hey, don't beat yourself up about that. This is a situation you have no control over. You're doing the best thing you can by remembering him and staying true to your beliefs."

"I just wish there was *something* I could do. I'd do anything."

Mr. Charleston folded his hands together, setting his newspaper aside. "If you wish, you could look at the library archives. But I must warn you. Don't lose yourself among history, Winter. It won't bode well for your future. It'll be hard, but you'll have to make peace with the injustice that your friend was served. Learning more about it may ease some of your concerns, I hope. But don't lose yourself along the way." He stood up, readying to leave.

"Wait!" Winter said, blocking his path. "Don't go yet." Mr. Charleston looked at her quizzically. Winter's gaze shifted down to his hands, which were holding a yellowed newspaper. "What's that?"

"It's the paper from the day my brother went missing."

"Would you mind if I borrowed it?"

Mr. Charleston withdrew himself, stepping back. "I'm sorry. I would let you borrow it, but this is the only copy left, and I'd like to keep it. It's not that I don't trust you to handle it properly. I just can't bear to lose the only reminder of him I have left." To Winter's surprise, he began to tear up.

Guilt clenched in Winter's stomach. "Oh, I'm so sorry," she consoled him. "I didn't mean it like that. I would never let it enter harm's way, but I understand. Besides, now that I know how much it means to you, I can't take it from you. It belongs to you."

Mr. Charleston wiped his eyes of any remaining tears. "You are truly one of the most honorable people I have ever met. Don't let anyone make you forget that."

Winter nodded. "I won't."

Mr. Charleston stood up. "Now, I hear it's somebody's birthday?"

Winter's face turned red. "Yep, it is."

"Happy birthday, dear. Now, what on *Earth* are you doing listening to the incoherent ramblings of an old man such as myself? Go off and have fun!" he exclaimed, kindly gesturing for her to leave.

Winter smiled. "I will. Thank you so much for everything. I really appreciate it."

"Go!"

She laughed. "Okay, if you insist!" And, with that, she ran off. Any ordinary passerby may think that Winter was running off in a hurry to go play with friends, or race around the town, pretending to be on a movie set. But both Winter and Mr. Charleston knew that not to be true. Winter gallivanted down the street, not because she was pretending to be the main character in a movie, nor because she was looking for her friends; she was going to the library archives to find out what had happened once and for all. She was filled with a familiar feeling, one that hadn't bloomed inside her for a long, long time. *Hope.*

Chapter Four

Winter finally reached the Town Hall. She walked up to the big brass door and knocked, feeling much too insignificant and out of place to use such an eloquent door knocker. At first, there was no answer. She waited a few moments.

Several minutes later, she heard the *click* of someone unlocking the door. It was opened by a gray-haired yet slightly balding dark-skinned man whom she recognized as the mayor, Mr. Winehall. He stepped outside, his smile beaming.

"Winter!" he announced. "I was just locking up. How nice to see you!"

"It's nice to see you too, Mr. Winehall."

He beamed. "What brings you here on this fine afternoon?"

"I was wondering if I could have a look at the newspaper archives."

His eyebrows creased in confusion. "The newspaper archives? What do you want to do there? I'm sure there are more exciting activities a young teenager such as yourself would rather spend her time doing on a fine summer day."

She smiled uneasily. "Actually, I wanted to go over some town history before school starts in a few weeks. I-I've been meaning to, um, learn more about the Salem witch trials for the history field trip." Her stomach clenched at the lie.

Mr. Winehall chuckled, shaking his head. "Our Winter. Always staying prepared. You truly do take after your parents. Your father would miss the school bus, too busy scouring his way through books, while your mother, bless her, would spend hours after school volunteering at the archives. I'm delighted that you're just as eager to learn as they were"

"So, I'm allowed to go in there?"

"Of course you are! I'm not gonna get in the way of a young scholar such as yourself. Follow me and I'll unlock it for you."

She did as he instructed, following his clean-cut footsteps along the wide corridor. Her eyes shifted to the various portraits on the walls, Mr. Winehall being the most recent addition among them. *These must be the former mayors of Redwick,* she thought. She wondered which ones were mayor when Richie and Amelia disappeared and whether they had believed them to be dead or not, but she didn't have time to look now.

They'd reached the end of the corridor. Mr. Winehall unlocked another fancy-looking door labeled "LIBRARY ARCHIVES."

"All yours. Be sure to finish by 5:00 pm." He lowered his voice to a whisper. "I'm supposed to close up at 3:00, but I'll make an exception for the future scholars of Redwick." He winked. "It'll be our little secret."

He noted the concerned look on Winter's face. "I wouldn't worry. It should *not* be a crime for a citizen of Redwick to enter the library past 3:00. How are you supposed to get your studying done? I've been trying to convince the City Council to keep it open until 7:00 pm, but I understand why that can be a safety concern. We may just have to settle for 5:00." He cleared his throat. "Anyways, I'll stop rambling about grownup problems I'm sure you don't want to hear about. Have a lovely time studying."

Her stomach twisted. He was such a kind man. She wanted to tell him the truth, but there was no good way to tell him. He wouldn't believe her. "Okay. Thank you so much!"

"I'd say have fun learning about Salem, but 'fun' isn't exactly the word I would use."

Winter chuckled softly. "Definitely not."

"Have a wonderful afternoon." He walked out the door, leaving Winter alone.

* * *

Faced with an overwhelming selection of filing cabinets, Winter didn't quite know where to start. She walked up to them, noticing that each year was arranged by date, making her life easier. She located the 1928 cabinet, searching for August. When she couldn't find anything helpful towards her search, she turned to the September folder, then on to October. Within minutes, she found what she was looking for.

The pages were yellow and covered in dust. She blew it off with a *whoosh* and began reading:

October 12th, 1928
Richard Charleston Still Not Found After 2 Month Search

After Richard Charleston's tragic disappearance just over two months ago, the Redwick Police have been looking far and wide, and they have not yet found him. The Police Department is seriously considering abandoning the search.

Winter could barely contain her anger. Who did these people think they were, dismissing an eleven-year-old kid's disappearance so quickly? Sure, Adam had been gone a year, but it didn't matter how much time had passed. He was still out there... right?

Maybe the reason Richie was never found alive was that they stopped looking for him long enough for him to die on his own. She shuddered at the thought, her heart going out to not just Richie, but Adam and Amelia, too.

Deciding the article contained nothing else of use for her search, she put it back in the *October 1928* folder, deciding instead to locate *August 1957*.

She found Amelia's article. This one was also yellowed and dusty, but much less so than Richie's as it dated thirty years later. She blew off the dust. Handling it gently, making sure not to crinkle any pages, she began to read:

August 26, 1957
Amelia Sunbury Disappearance Remains a Mystery

The whereabouts of Amelia Sunbury, the young, sweet, scholarly girl we all know and love, remain unknown. After her tragic disappearance two weeks ago, the Redwick Police still have yet to find her. Besides the discovery of her red polka dot handkerchief at the scene of the crime, which has been returned to her parents, there is nothing new to report.

Winter's hope deflated. Had she come all the way out here for nothing?

She sighed. With great disappointment, she put the article away.

To make things worse, the clock chimed 4:00 pm. She was running out of time. "Great, now what?" she asked herself out loud. She found herself returning to the 1928 drawer, checking the later months for any updates on Richie. She scanned the pages of each day's newspaper for Richie's name, the clock *tick-tick-tick*ing.

Finally, she found one that mentioned his name:

December 9, 1928
Richard Charleston Legally Declared Dead

Five months later, the case has finally been closed: Richard Charleston is dead. His body hasn't been found; however, it has been long enough that he would've died out on his own, hence the search has been abandoned. We are filled with great sadness to say goodbye to such a young, free-spirited child. We send our utmost condolences to the Charleston family.

Winter held in a scream. "If his body wasn't found," she said to herself through gritted teeth, "Then WHY did they think he was DEAD?"

She couldn't take it anymore. She was absolutely dumbfounded and disappointed in her hometown. The sheer willingness of Redwick to abandon all hope and label something as tragic as a child's disappearance as a death rather than continuing the investigation astounded her.

She decided to leave the archives, angrier than she'd been before, all hope lost.

Out of the blue, she remembered something Mr. Charleston had said to her earlier. *You are truly one of the most honorable people I have ever met. Don't let anyone make you forget that.*

Winter felt guilty for even considering giving up. Looking one last time couldn't hurt. She headed over to the 1957 folder, searching for a closure article about Amelia's legally declared death, instead finding something rather unusual:

September 1, 1957
Could the Disappearances of Amelia Sunbury and Richard Charleston Have Paranormal Origin?

Thirty years ago, Richard Charleston was legally declared dead. Just like Amelia Sunbury, he disappeared at the Redwick summer carnival. Citizens have petitioned against the carnival running in the future, but the likelihood of the petition being passed is unlikely as the carnival is Redwick's most beloved tourist attraction. We wouldn't want to lose our beloved tourists, right?

The Police are still searching for Amelia. She was last seen at the Redwick summer carnival. While this may seem like a coincidence, take note of this: both of them were rumored to have witnessed paranormal phenomena.

The Sunbury family have kindly agreed to discuss their daughter's tragic disappearance. In an interview conducted by a Redwick Police officer, who shall remain nameless, Mr. and Mrs. Sunbury noted that in the days prior to her disappearance, Amelia talked about hearing a strange "whispering" noise. If you are a true citizen of Redwick, you may or may not remember the disappearance of poor Richard Charleston. For all of you newer Redwick members, Richard disappeared in 1928, but he was never found. His parents mentioned that he also heard a strange "whispering" voice in his head, but these claims were never put in the newspaper due to suspected evil origins.

Times have changed, Redwick. It's time to tell the real story. Could it be that these two children were sick and both heard strange voices in their heads, losing themselves to their mental delusions?

Winter grimaced in disgust at the last sentence. Why would the author of this news article *assume* that Richie and Amelia were mentally ill because they both heard voices in their heads, then spread their opinion even wider by declaring it to the public? Why could some people be so cynical?

And what did they mean by *whispering?*

Then it hit her.

The voice in the diner.

Could it be...

No. It couldn't be true. She shook her head, dismissing the thought.

The clock chimed 5:00 pm. It was time for her to go.

Chapter Five

Winter left the town hall, transitioning from a dark, unlit room to bright, blinding sunshine. It was like she was entering another world.

Mr. Winehall popped up behind her, his smile so large it could've come from a clown in a horror movie. "Well, look who studied until the last minute! Honestly, Winter, I am so proud of you."

"Thank you, Mr. Winehall, but I should really get going. Have a lovely evening." She turned to leave, eager to get home in time for dinner.

"One last thing before you go," Mr. Winehall noted, pointing to her right. Winter turned to the direction he was pointing in. "Have you noticed the town message board? It's new! It's about time that we had one! We have almost every other small-town cliché -- a diner, a mayor, a town hall, town meetings -- it's simply unacceptable that we didn't have a message board! Well, I'm heading back inside. The work day isn't quite over... but I wish it was!" He laughed. "Just kidding. I love my job. Have a nice evening!"

"You too!" she responded as he walked back inside.

Winter decided that dinner could wait. She hadn't noticed the message board before, and she loved seeing new things pop up around town. She skipped over to it and saw a plethora of fliers; pink ones, blue ones, yellow ones, white ones. She read them; most of them were advertisements, like the new pizza shop opening or the discounted sale at the antique shop on Woodridge, but there was one flier that stood out among the others:

ANNUAL TRAVELING CARNIVAL RETURNING
TO REDWICK

WELL, FOLKS, IT'S HAPPENING. IT'S TIME FOR
THE BELOVED TRAVELING SUMMER CARNIVAL
TO RETURN TO REDWICK. ADORED BY ALL,
THIS CARNIVAL HAS EVERYTHING A KID
COULD EVER WANT -- AND ADULTS, TOO (PSST...
PARENTS: MOST OF THE FOOD STANDS SELL
ALCOHOL)! THERE ARE A WIDE VARIETY OF
RIDES, FROM MERRY-GO-ROUNDS TO THE
MIRROR MAZE TO "THE TWISTER." PICK YOUR
POISON! AND YOU WON'T WANT TO MISS THE
FUNNEL CAKES -- THEY'RE TO DIE FOR.
CITIZENS OF REDWICK, PREPARE FOR THE
TIME OF YOUR LIFE.

DATES: AUGUST 8TH-16TH

The traveling carnival. Winter hadn't been there since she was with
Adam on the day he disappeared. Even before he vanished, it hadn't
been much fun. She was too young for the "big kid" rides and too old
for the "little kid" rides. The only attraction that sounded interesting
to her was the mirror maze. *It must be new,* she thought, for she had
never seen it. *How strange.* It wasn't usual for the carnival to add new
attractions.

She pondered this for a moment but dismissed the thought. After
all, wouldn't her parents tell her to not waste any more time dwelling
on things she shouldn't?

* * *

There was one more thing Winter wanted to do before she went home: make a quick stop by the theater. *Dinner can wait,* she thought, her curiosity overpowering her impatience. This was all the time she would get alone for the day, so she had to make the most of it.

Within minutes, Winter had arrived at the old movie theater. It looked just as it always had, the once flashing light bulbs jutting out from the sign. *Redwick Theater,* the sign read. Winter sighed, reminiscing a time she'd never known.

She glanced at the ticket booth, imagining it had been in high demand during the grand opening of the theater. Now, it was empty. Abandoned. Tossed aside to make room for newer things, like televisions, where people can easily watch any old movie with just a *click.* Winter wished things had turned out differently -- that modern technology wasn't advanced enough to result in the closing of the Redwick Theater.

She entered the theater, enjoying the coolness that the darkness offered. It wasn't pitch black; no, not quite. There was just enough light so she wasn't blinded, but she could still see. While she wasn't completely disconnected from the world, she could still briefly step into the past.

She ran her hands over the patchy fabric of chair after chair, soaking up the safety of the theater. She passed seat after seat, looking for her favorite spot. After brushing countless comfy seats, she'd reached her destination: seats 2A and 2B.

2B was hers, and hers only. 2A was Adam's, and 2B was hers. The two came there every Friday after school, ice creams in hand (from Roseberg's, of course. Where else?). They would sit there for hours, joking about staying there forever, or trading their deepest, darkest secrets. She sat in the all-too-familiar chair, relishing the cool, soft leather feel. She closed her eyes.

Shhhhhh, hissed a familiar voice.

Winter jumped, eyes open. "Hello? Who's there?"

No response.

"I'm warning you, I'm armed," she lied. It wasn't entirely a lie. She had a Hello Kitty backpack. She knew she probably wasn't supposed to be here, so whoever had entered the vicinity would likely ask for her removal.

I'm sorry if I startled you, young one, came its quiet response. Winter couldn't tell where it was coming from. She looked around, but there was no one in sight.

"W-who are you?" she asked, her voice shaking.

It paused for a moment. *Don't you remember? We met earlier. At the diner.*

Winter gaped. "It's you."

I'm not quite sure whom you're referring to.

"You told me to order strawberry ice cream. And you know about Adam"

Ah, yes. That would be me.

There was a long pause. "Who are you?" Winter inquired, growing impatient.

Another pause. *I am no one, yet I am also many people.*

Winter's eyebrows furrowed. "Huh?"

Silence.

"Hello? I'm still talking to you," Winter responded a little too loudly, the reflection of her voice echoing back at her from around the theater.

Minutes passed, but the voice never responded. Winter hopelessly wondered if she had imagined it all. Maybe it was because of her loneliness.

Stop. Don't think like that, she told herself. With a deep breath, she stood up, deciding to look for the source of the voice, recognizing that if no one else was there, she was definitely crazy.

She walked around the theater, stepping onto the stage and whisking her way between seats. It couldn't have all been in her head, could it? What if she really was going crazy? It wasn't normal for a kid her age to be friendless. *You've finally admitted it, Winter. You have no friends. You're all alone.*

Maybe loneliness isn't what's making you crazy. Maybe you're already crazy and that's *why you're lonely.*

"Stop beating yourself up. It's fine. You're okay. You'll-you'll be okay." She took a deep breath.

She left the theater, ready for pizza, popcorn, cake, a family movie marathon, and a good night's sleep.

Chapter Six

Winter ran through the mirror maze, panting. She had been running for hours. Or had it been days? Either way, she'd been running for far too long.

She was on the verge of consciousness, her exhaustion nearly overpowering her will to keep going. But she couldn't give up. Not yet. She had to do something. Had to find *something.*

But what was she looking for?

An exit! *Hissed a familiar voice in her head.*

"An exit to where?" she exclaimed.

A new place, *whispered the voice.*

"What kind of place?"

A better place. Some place where you can be free. Where you *will* be free.

"What do you mean?"

But it was too late. The voice had vanished.

"Hello? Say something!"

Silence.

Determined to find the source of the voice, she ran through the maze. She glanced at her infinite reflections, taking note of the infinite Winters.

Eventually, she came upon an opening: a break in the glass. Only it wasn't just a break. It was a-

* * *

Winter rubbed the sleep out of her eyes. She felt dizzy, failing to recognize her surroundings. Blinking a few times, she readjusted her focus from dream to reality.

It had been the most curious dream... the problem was she couldn't remember exactly what had happened.

"Winter!" her mom's voice called up the stairs. "Time for breakfast!"

"Coming!"

She ran down the stairs, greeted by the warming aroma of freshly cooked pancakes, her favorite breakfast food... her parents had to be up to something.

She entered the kitchen, her dad already seated at the table, happily piling pancake after pancake onto his plate.

"Would you like to go to the town carnival?" her mom asked as she slid a freshly cooked warm pancake onto her plate from the pan. Winter buttered it and poured a little bit (okay, a lot) of maple syrup on it.

"Um..."

Her mom sighed. "Honey, we know it might be difficult for you, seeing as that's where..." she hesitated.

"Where Adam disappeared?" her father questioned through a mouthful of pancake.

Her mom shot him an accusatory look. "Yes. That." She lowered her voice. "Honestly, David, could you be any less subtle?" She sighed. "It's your choice, honey. We won't go if you aren't ready."

"You don't want to miss all the fun, right? There'll be games and rides, and I heard they might have funnel cake this year," her dad said, not trying to hide his enthusiasm. Her mom rolled her eyes, letting out a soft giggle.

Winter knew how much her parents loved the carnival. She couldn't disappoint them again. Besides, she wanted to investigate the mirror maze. "Alright. We can go."

"Yippee!" her father shouted. "Uh, I mean, alright. Okay. Doesn't matter. It's not like I'll have any fun. I'm totally not super looking forward to this." He winked at Winter.

Her mother, clearly impressed, broke into a grin. "Yay! I'm glad. It'll be so much fun for you! Now that you're thirteen, you can go on 'The Twister!'"

"There's no way I'm going on *that*." Her family laughed.

* * *

"Come on, Winter, it's time to go!" her mother shouted up the stairs as Winter threw on her socks and shoes.

"Coming!" She quickly glanced at the clock. 8:55. She shouldn't have slept in, but she couldn't help it. She'd been tossing and turning all night, worried about the whispering. She still had so many questions. Why did Richie disappear? Where did he go? Did he die? Had anyone else heard the whispering? But she didn't have time to worry right now.

She was supposed to wake up at 8:00 am so she could eat breakfast and get to the carnival by 9:00 am when it opened. Now, the carnival was five mere minutes away from opening. She would have to deal with the mid-morning rush. She glanced at the clock again. 8:56. *Never mind. Four.*

"We're gonna be late!" her mom shouted.

"Ugh, I'm coming!" Winter shouted back. She quickly looked over her outfit in the mirror: a pink Roseburg's Diner t-shirt, navy blue jean shorts, and black converse shoes. Simple and cute.

She grabbed her phone and backpack and ran down the stairs, panting.

"I'm-h-here-now," she said, breathing heavily. "Sorry. Slept in."

Her mom sighed. "It's alright. Here, have this on the way." She handed her a fresh peach and a granola bar.

She grabbed them, munching on the granola bar as she opened the car door.

* * *

"We're here!" her dad announced triumphantly.

Winter shielded her eyes, blocking out the sun. "Eww, it's so hot. Why can't it be fall already?"

"Winter, please try to enjoy the carnival. It's a lovely day," her mom said happily. "We'll have to buy some tickets. Although I did bring our coupon from winning Ring Toss last year. We get one free ride!"

"You always were a star thrower, Catherine."

Winter's mom blushed. "Oh, stop!" she said, mock-slapping him.

"No, I'm serious. I used to come to all of your softball games. To see you, of course. Not that I had any real interest in the game. You're still just as amazing as you were back then," he said, planting a kiss on her cheek.

"Eww," Winter groaned.

Her parents chuckled. "Sorry, Winter. I'm just so deeply in love with your mother that I can't help myself."

Her mom's face reddened, lightning as she turned to her daughter. "Winter, what would you like to do first?"

Winter surveyed her surroundings. She noticed several familiar places, such as the red and white striped circus tent (after meeting the new creepy clown last year, she vowed to never step foot in there again), the funhouse, the Helter-Skelter, and the snack bar.

"Do you have anything in mind?" her dad asked her. "Personally, I have my eye on the snack bar. *They're serving alcohol*." He whispered this last part to her mom.

"You guys can go there. I'll catch up with you later."

Her parents shared a worried look.

"Relax. It's not like I'm going to look for something Adam-related. I'm over that now." She was definitely *not* over it.

Her parents relaxed.

"Alright, sweetie," her mom said gently, handing her a $10 bill. "Here's $10. Use it for whatever you want. Just have some fun! Goodness knows we all need it."

Her dad checked his watch. "It's 9:21 now. Try and meet us at the food court no later than noon, okay, kiddo?"

"I will."

"Don't be long!" her mom shouted.

"I won't!" She ran off, her parents' silhouettes getting smaller and smaller.

Little did she know, it would feel like an eternity before she saw either of them again.

Chapter Seven

Winter wandered around the carnival looking for something to do. *Games, no. Snacks, no. Rides? Maybe.*

She looked around for a ride of interest. She didn't want something too intense after just finishing breakfast. Definitely not *The Twister.* But not something too babyish, either. She was thirteen, after all.

As she pondered what to do, she noticed a shiny flash out of the corner of her left eye. Maybe it was a ride? She turned and saw the mirror maze.

Curious, she wandered towards it, still confused by the "no children allowed" sign. What was the point of having an attraction that children couldn't even enter?

She faced the entrance, squinting from the bright glare of the sun's reflection on the mirrors. It appeared to be empty. She couldn't even find a ticket booth; how was she supposed to get a ticket to go inside?

"A mirror maze!" a little boy near her shouted, pointing. "Mommy, can I go in?"

"What mirror maze? I don't see one."

"Mommy, it's right there!" He pointed towards Winter. "Look, there's a girl standing near it!"

"Honey, there's no mirror maze." The boy whined. "I can see a girl, but I don't see a mirror maze. You must be imagining it."

This struck Winter as strange; how could this woman not see the mirror maze? It was right in plain sight.

"Fineee, but can I get cotton candy now?" the boy whined.

"Sure, honey. But no more sugar after that!" his mom replied as she walked off with her son.

Winter watched as they walked off. How strange... why couldn't the mom see it, but her son could? It stood out to Winter solely because of the sun's reflection, making it hard not to notice... surely the mom had seen it? Winter frowned.

Why the long face? a strange, familiar voice whispered.

Winter turned around, looking for the source of the voice. She had an inkling as to what it was, but didn't know where it was coming from. "Who are you, and why are you here?"

Only one way to tell, Winter Barnes.

"And what's that?"

I think you already know. The voice echoed inside of the maze.

"Are-are you in there? In the mirror maze?"

Silence.

"Only one thing to do." She took a deep breath and walked in.

* * *

Winter looked around at the dozens upon dozens of mirrors around her. She gazed into her reflection: a soft expression was imprinted upon her face, her amber eyes gentle and her mouth in a straight line. She looked over her noticeable features: her olive brown skin, her poofy black hair flowing down to her shoulders, and her little round nose that she criticized so much but everyone else seemed to love.

Will you stop staring at your reflection and focus on what's really important here? The voice echoed.

"Yes, sorry. I need to find my way to the other side, don't I?"

Just follow the maze and you'll find your way home.

"Okay."

Home? What did it mean by *home?* She dismissed the thought.

She wandered around the maze, turning this way and that. It seemed to be never-ending. She navigated the twists and turns, failing to find the exit.

It felt like it had been hours. Frustrated, Winter checked her phone. No signal. It was 9:28.

"9:28? But that's impossible." She expected a response from the voice, but there was none. "How can it be the same time that I came in? It's been at least half an hour."

Mirror mazes weren't impossible. Why was this one so difficult to navigate?

Well, Winter, there's only one thing you can do, she said to herself. *Wander around until you find your way out.*

And she did just that. Several minutes later, she'd still made little progress. She was beginning to get frustrated.

"Unidentified voice, why abandon me when I need you most?"

Alas, my dear Winter, I would never abandon you. Why would you even think such a thing?

"You're back! Can you tell me which way to go?"

You're almost there. Just keep following your reflection until you find something out of the ordinary. Trust me.

"What do you mean?"

No response.

"Fine. I guess I'll just keep going. There's nothing else I can do."

She walked around for a few minutes, when all of a sudden, she smelled something. *Popcorn.*

She kept going, the scent remaining. She was heading in the right direction -- she had to be.

Finally, the twists of the maze came to an end. There was a long stretch of mirrors in front of her, leading to light at the end of the tunnel. An end to this never-ending maze.

More scents were added to the mix. Cotton candy, hot dogs, churros...

Just then, she heard the faint sound of birds chirping, feeling a warm, summer breeze brush against her face.

She kept walking.

Faster, and

Faster, and
Faster, and
Stop.
She'd reached the end.

Chapter Eight

Winter walked out of the tunnel into a wide, sunny carnival scene. She was greeted with the familiar aroma of popping kernels, grilled hot dogs, and freshly fried churros that had appeared in the mirror maze. It felt like home.

She studied her surroundings. It was like she'd come back to the carnival, except it seemed like an entirely different era altogether. While she spotted the familiar carnival sights, like the Ferris wheel, rides, and snack bars, there were some periodical oddities. For starters, everyone nowadays used Spotify or Pandora or streaming services like that, but neither of those were present. There was a record player present, but it was playing an old jazz song she didn't recognize. Secondly, everything looked outdated. There were very few cars, and the cars that were parked alongside the curb looked practically ancient.

Winter crinkled her eyebrows, wondering why everything seemed so off-kilter.

It's like I'm in another time period, she thought.

You never know, a familiar voice whispered; although, this time, the voice wasn't just in her head; it was all around her, echoing throughout this yearning-to-be-explored world.

"Hello? Is this real, or am I imagining things?" Winter uttered out loud.

Oh, it's very real, the unidentifiable voice replied.

Winter gaped. "Who are you? What are you? Where are you?"

I'm not anyone. I'm not anything. I'm just me.

Winter faltered. "Do you have a name?"

No.

"Well, how do I know what to call you?"

It said nothing.

"Where are you? You've been talking to me ever since..."

Ever since what?

"I'm not sure if I should say it. It'll make me sound even crazier."

Go on, say it. There's no harm in guessing. You're safe here. I will not judge you.

Winter relented. "Ever since I traveled back in time." She hesitated. "That is what happened, right? I mean, look at the old cars. Look at the record player. This can't be the 21st century."

You're right. This isn't the 21st century.

"Well then, what year is it?"

You'll just have to guess.

"Seriously? *More* guessing?" No response. "Fine. I'd guess-"

"Why are you talking to yourself?" an unfamiliar voice pressed. "Seriously, you look like you're talking to a ghost."

Winter turned around and spotted a young boy. He was tan, as if he'd lived under the sun all his life. His face was spotted with freckles. He had shiny but messy dirty-blond hair that glowed as he walked through the sun and darkened as he walked through the shadows.

He held out his hand. Winter shook it warily. "Hi, I'm Richie."

Winter immediately let go. "Richie..."

"Richie Charleston. Have I met you before? You look familiar."

Winter stared at him. *Mr. Charleston's missing brother. It's him.*

"Are you gonna keep staring at me, or are you gonna answer my question?"

"Right. Sorry. No, we haven't met."

"Then why do you look so familiar?"

"I don't know. I guess I just do."

Richie crossed his arms, looking puzzled. "Hmm, okay. What's your name?"

"Winter. Winter Barnes."

"What a weird name..."

Winter rolled her eyes. "Thanks."

"I don't mean it as an insult. It's actually cool. I just mean it sounds familiar."

"Why?"

"I dunno, it's just..." he trailed off. After a moment, he gasped. "It's you!" He ran off, not saying another word.

Winter stared after him, perplexed. How could Richie *possibly* know her?

Winter located a wooden bench. She sat down and looked around: no cigarette butts sticking out of sidewalk cracks, no gum stuck on the ground; nothing. How could this world be so perfect?

I need to figure out where I am. Or, better yet, when *I am,* Winter thought. *Maybe there's someone I could ask? I could ask Richie when he gets back. Although, that might seem weird...*

She didn't really care. Everything about this day had been weird enough. She decided to sit down and wait it out.

As she had no way to track the time, she had no idea how long it'd been when Richie actually came back, dragging along a partner.

"Winter? Is that you?" a familiar voice uttered.

Winter's heart fluttered. She thought she'd never hear that voice again. She looked up.

Her lower jaw dropped open. It was Adam.

Chapter Nine

Adam looked just the same as he had the last time she saw him, except that his freckles were highlighted by his recent tan.

Adam waved his hand in her face. "Hello? Earth to Winter. Do you copy?"

Winter was unable to move, frozen to the spot. *It can't be Adam,* she thought. *It just can't be... it's too good to be true.*

"She wasn't like this when I first saw her," Richie butted in. "Actually, she was talking to a ghost. Or herself, I don't know which. We'd better be careful with this one. Just kidding. We're all an odd bunch. She'll fit in with us just fine."

"Slow down, Richie. You're overwhelming her," Adam said. "Winter, I know this might seem like a lot, like it's too good to be true, but it's me. It's really me."

Winter questioned it no further. "It's you. I can't believe it's really you." They embraced, the hug welcoming and familiar. She was home.

"Well, this is awkward," Richie said.

Winter and Adam broke apart.

"Sorry," Adam said. "I just can't believe you're here."

Winter smiled. She felt as if a weight had been lifted off of her shoulders.

"You've been gone for a year." There was no use avoiding the subject.

Adam immediately paled. "Yeah, I guess I have." He hesitated, looking down at his shoes, clearly not wanting to touch the topic.

"How did you get here?" Winter asked gently.

"I-I don't know. I can't remember."

Winter furrowed her brow. *How could Adam not remember something so important?*

"You can't remember?"

Adam shook his head. "No. I'm sorry."

"No, it's fine. I'm just glad you're here." She hugged him again.

"Ugh, stop, that's gross," Richie exclaimed.

Adam laughed, pulling out of the hug. "What's wrong with hugging someone you haven't seen in forever?"

"I guess that's true," Richie relented.

Winter remembered that she had to find out what she so desperately needed to know. "Where are we?"

Richie shrugged. "Paradise." Adam hesitated, then nodded. *That was strange,* Winter thought. *Why did he hesitate?*

"Are we dead?" Winter asked, mildly worried.

Adam shook his head. "I think we'd know if we were dead, Winter."

"But..."

"Stop worrying so much!" Richie said. "We're here to have fun, so let's go have fun!"

Winter relaxed. "What do you do for fun around here?"

"Oh, usually we go to the theater-"

Winter jumped. "The theater!" she squealed. "Let's go there!"

Adam and Richie opened their eyes. "Wow," Adam noted. "I'm glad you're so excited about it. It's good to see you happy and carefree again." He smiled. Winter thought she could detect the slightest hint of uneasiness in his eyes, but dismissed it; what reason would Adam have to be uneasy, anyways? She was probably just imagining it.

"You'll love it," Richie said, despite only knowing her for a few minutes. "It's totally new. It just opened last year."

Winter remembered that she'd wanted to ask what year it was. "And last year was..."

"1927," Richie said. "It's 1928. Don't you know that?"

"Relax, Richie. She just got here. How would she know that?"

"Oh, right," Richie replied, his face turning red.

Wow. So, she was in the 1920s. That explained the record player and the old cars. And -- the theater! Oh, how she'd yearned to see it when it first opened. Her wildest dreams had come true.

"Uh, guys?" Winter reminded them. "The theater?"

Richie brightened. "Oh, yeah! Let's go! We'll take you there."

The three of them headed over to the theater. "What's showing?" Winter asked eagerly, all prior suspicion forgotten.

"I have no clue. I guess it'll be a surprise."

Winter felt happier than ever. She loved surprises. Maybe this world wasn't so strange after all.

* * *

"Look," Richie shouted, pointing across the street. "There's Amelia!"

That name rang a bell. Amelia... she'd heard that name before...

"You'll love her," Adam added. "Do you want to go meet her?"

"Yeah, of course," Winter said, her mind drifting off as they walked. Where had she heard that name?

Before she knew it, they'd reached Amelia, and Richie was already speaking again. "Winter, meet Amelia. Amelia, meet Winter,"

Winter looked at Amelia. She was older than her, maybe fourteen or fifteen. Her face was bright, her smile warm. She noticed two hidden dimples pop out of the corners of her cheeks. Her strawberry blonde hair whirled in the subtle summer breeze, creating the illusion that she was a movie star whose hair artificially blew in the wind, yet it was real. It was *all* real. She wore a medium-length off-white dress with red polka dots that contrasted the gentle cream background. She wore black flats that looked like they came out of a different era. *They* did *come out of a different era,* Winter noted.

"It's a pleasure to meet you," Amelia declared, shaking Winter's hand. She had a firm but nonassertive grip. She seemed friendly.

"It's nice to meet you, too," Winter replied.

Winter couldn't quite pinpoint what was so familiar about her. Could it be her handshake? *No, too unique.* Could it be her hair? *No, too mesmerizingly abstract.* Could it be...

"I wish I had my handkerchief," Amelia lamented. "The breeze keeps blowing dirt in my eye."

Something clicked.

Amelia Sunbury, Winter remembered.

"What did it look like?" she asked. Amelia gave her a funny look. "I mean, maybe I can help you find it? I might've seen it along the way."

Amelia relented. "I can't quite remember. I think it was striped. Or plaid. Or filled with flowers. Something along those lines."

"Was it polka-dotted?"

Amelia's eyes widened. "Yes! That's right!" Her shoulders drooped. "How did you know that?"

"Oh, just a guess." She gestured to Amelia's dress. "You seem to really like polka dots."

Amelia laughed politely. "Yes, I do. It's my favorite pattern." She paused. "If you find it, would you mind returning it to me? It would be nice to see something that reminds me of home."

"Why don't you just go home?" Winter suggested. "Nothing's stopping you."

The three kids paused.

Winter's eyebrows crinkled. "Did I say something wrong?"

"No," Richie began. "You didn't. We just-" He paused. "Winter, there's something you should know." He nodded at Adam, egging him to continue the thought.

"We can't remember where we're from. All we remember is here. There are some exceptions, though. We haven't forgotten everything. For example, I remember you, Winter Barnes... but I can't remember how we met or where I know you from."

Winter felt like she'd been stabbed in the back. How could he not remember?

"Adam, you're scaring me." She stared at him intensely, as if she were to look away, he would disappear again.

"Why? Winter, you look like you're in shock."

"How could you not remember Redwick?" she nearly whispered.

Adam tilted his head. "That sounds familiar. I think…" His eyes widened. "Oh, right, Redwick! The town!"

Winter nodded. "What else can you remember?"

Adam paused. "Well, I remember you."

Winter smiled.

"We're best friends."

Winter smiled harder. "You said *we*."

Adam looked up at her. "Of course I did. We'll always be best friends."

"Um, hello? What about me?" Richie asked.

"I haven't forgotten about you, Richie," Adam laughed. "I can have more than one best friend, right?"

"Sure, but you can only have one bestest friend. Obviously," Richie added. They all laughed.

"We can all be best friends," Adam suggested. Winter nodded. She was happy with that. She felt like she never wanted to leave this moment. She felt like she couldn't possibly be happier.

Chapter Ten

"The theater is just across the street. Wanna head over?" Adam asked.

"Of course! Why wouldn't I?" Winter asked. She was suddenly in a brightened state of indescribable happiness. She felt at ease. She believed that she could only ever feel this way *here.*

"It's good to see you like this," Amelia commented. "You seemed cautious and, honestly, kind of off-kilter earlier. I'm glad you're alright now."

"I'm feeling great!" Winter exclaimed, smiling wide. "Well, what are we waiting for? Let's go to the theater!"

* * *

"What's playing today?" Winter asked.

"Some silent film. Not quite sure what it's called, but you should get used to it. They play the same one every day," Adam said.

"What fun is that?" Winter asked.

Richie looked at her as if she'd grown a second head. "Why wouldn't you want to watch the same movie over and over again if it was good?"

Winter paused, then nodded. "I get that. I normally like to try new things... but there are some things that I want to always stay the same."

Adam smiled. "That's why we love it here. Some things change -- like you, for instance. I haven't seen you in forever. But it's the little things that count. I don't know what I'd do if I couldn't enjoy myself like this every day." His smile was so big it was starting to scare her. It looked... fake. Like it was forced.

Winter shot a concerned look at Adam. He returned the gesture. Winter plastered a grin on her face, mirroring the one Adam had had before. "I think I'm going to like it here."

"I'm so glad you like it," Amelia said.

The four strolled down the street, Winter and Adam in front and Amelia and Richie behind. They were like peas in a pod.

Winter knew she was on the oh-so-familiar Woodridge Lane, but everything seemed a little bit... *different*. In her Redwick, the street was filled with people entering and exiting shops, grabbing their go-to coffee before they headed out to work, simply going about their daily routine. In this Redwick, the street was empty and free, seeming cleaner than ever before; she noted that all traces of pollution seemed to have vanished. It was a pleasant odor.

But that didn't stop her suspicions from creeping in.

Why did everything feel so familiar yet so different?

The world began to blur. She felt dizzy.

Winter, a familiar voice rasped.

She spun around, knocking straight into Adam.

He stared at her. "Winter, are you alright?"

"I-what?"

"I said, are you okay? You looked a little lost there."

"Y-yes. I'm fine."

Adam, not quite convinced, crinkled his eyebrows. "Alright. Good. That's good." He cleared his throat. They continued walking.

"We're here!" Richie announced moments later.

Winter's eyes traveled up to her and Adam's beloved theater. She couldn't exactly say nothing had changed; this time, the theater was actually up and running. The *REDWICK THEATER* sign glowed, its flashing letters popping out at her from above. The aroma of buttery popcorn and sweet cotton candy enveloped her in a warm embrace. It was just as she'd imagined.

"Wow, this place is incredible!" Winter remarked.

"Yeah, it sure is great," Amelia said.

Something pricked at Winter's conscience. "Wait a minute. How are we going to pay for this? I didn't bring any money."

Everyone turned to look at her.

"Money? Seriously, Winter, you're so naïve," Richie pointed out.

"Hey, be nice," Amelia said. Richie looked down at his shoes, ashamed. Winter noted that Amelia had the upper hand when it came to Richie's attitude. "Winter, everything's free here. We don't use money. I can't even remember the last time I used it."

Winter gaped. "No money? How do you pay for everything?"

"Like I said, everything is free."

"Why?"

"I don't know. I haven't really thought about it."

Winter gaped, not quite sure what to make of this profound discovery. "Well. That settles it. This is officially the best place ever."

* * *

They walked into the theater, greeted with the comforting sounds of kernels popping in the machine. Films played softly in the background, the sound accompanied by the whirring of tapes and the projecting of projectors.

Winter felt guilty about not buying tickets, but knew that she wouldn't be held responsible here. Whatever *here* was.

"Heya, kiddos!" the popcorn machine vendor exclaimed. His eyes were wide open, his eyebrows rose higher than they were supposed to, and his mouth formed an O-shape. Spooky. "Welcome to the Redwick Theater! What can I get ya? Popcorn? Cotton candy? Soda? We've got it all!"

"We'll have... everything!" Richie screamed dramatically, jaw open.

Amelia rolled her eyes. "I'll just have a soda, thanks."

"C'mon, Mills. Don't you at least want popcorn?"

A grin spread across her face. "Alright. I'll have a small popcorn, please."

"What about you, little lady?" the hyper vendor asked her.

She snuck a sly glance at Richie. "I'll have one of everything."

"Great! And you, young man?" He turned to Adam. "Your usual?"

"My usual."

The vendor nodded, preparing their orders. Within no time, he turned back around and handed everyone a soda, Adam a soda and popcorn, and Richie and Winter one of everything.

"Awesome," Richie beamed, already digging into his popcorn. "C'mon, wet's go insiwde," he said with his mouth full. Amelia rolled her eyes, trying to hide her smile.

The four of them headed into the theater. Winter couldn't hide her bursting excitement and anticipation at *finally* being able to watch a film in her theater. Yes, *her* theater. That sounded right.

She waltzed into the room, inhaling the aroma of the crisp, brand-new leather seats mingled together with their popcorn and cotton candy. The film hadn't started yet, so the theater was silent except for the *crack-crack-crack*ling of their sodas. The seats were soft, releasing any anxiety Winter may have had. The atmosphere was calm and relaxing as if she was always meant to belong here.

"Hurry up!" Richie called out, oblivious to how loud he was. "It's starting!"

They ran over as if to claim the front row seats, despite them being the only ones in the theater.

"This one's mine!" Richie shouted. *He's so loud,* Winter thought, smiling to herself.

Amelia and Adam followed Richie, sitting in the front row. Winter froze. *Why wasn't he in row 2 with her?* "Adam, what about 2A and 2B?"

Adam crinkled his eyebrows. "What about them? We can just sit here."

Winter felt like her world had tilted.

"We always sit here."

Adam stared blankly at her like a deer in headlights. "Does it matter? If it's really important to you, we can sit there." He began to walk towards her.

"No-no. It's fine," Winter said, shoulders drooping. Why was Adam acting so weird? First, he didn't remember how they'd met, then he'd forgotten Redwick, and now this? She began to feel sick to her stomach.

Winter sat next to Adam in a seat that *wasn't* 2B. She tried to ignore it, but she couldn't brush off the feeling of unease stirring inside her.

A few minutes into the film, Winter got out of her seat. "I need to use the bathroom. I'll be right back." Before anyone could interject or say anything, she swiftly headed out of the theater.

Now, where is the bathroom? she said to herself. She wandered around the theater, unsure of where to go. She noticed the silence. The stillness. It felt like a fever dream. Winter pinched herself to make sure she wasn't dreaming.

She headed down the dimly lit hallway and found her way to the bathroom. It looked like every other movie theater bathroom, but somehow *neater*. The charcoal-gray tiled floors were freshly polished, projecting Winter's reflection right back at her; but that wasn't what caught her eye. What caught her eye was the mirror. She wasn't just staring at herself: her light brown skin, her hazel eyes, her fluffy black hair. There was a substantially large smudge covering nearly half of the surface.

She stared at it for a bit, noticing its barely discernible contours and edges. It looked almost like a doodle, or a sketch, but not quite right.

Winter grabbed a tissue, keeping her eyes on the shape. As she studied it, the lights began to flicker. Light after light flickered on and off. Mere seconds later, they stopped.

Hello, Winter Barnes, the thing said.

She jumped, turning around, catching nothing in her line of sight. Perplexed, she looked back at the mirror. It was gone.

"What a strange thing..." Winter mused to herself, brushing it off like it was no big deal. She was used to her life feeling off-kilter. Even if it did involve a talking smudge on the bathroom mirror.

She turned around and the smudge was directly behind her, facing her, looking her in the eye.

Welcome home. I've been waiting for you.

Chapter Eleven

Winter stared at the figure. It was there, but also not there. It had an otherworldly sense to it -- like a living nightmare. She couldn't make out its features. It looked like a mix between a scribble and a smudge of charcoal. She honestly couldn't tell what it was.

"What-" she began, realizing that she would probably sound rude. "I mean, *who* are you?"

Silence.

More silence.

Was that the wrong question to ask? Winter pondered.

It blinked at her. She stared at its eyes. They were little white circles -- it really did look like a doodle. It was almost as if it *was* a sketch of some sort. She walked towards it, arm extended, her other arm ready to brace herself in case of an emergency.

"Do you mind if I touch you?" she asked, wondering if it was transparent. "Let me know if you aren't comfortable with this." She didn't know what would happen; was it a ghost? Would her hand pass right through? She took a deep breath and plunged her hand through the other side. Nothing.

I'm not a ghost if that's what you're thinking.

Winter jumped, wondering if it had read her thoughts. "You startled me."

I'm sorry. I didn't mean to frighten you. She relaxed.

"Are you the one who's been talking to me these past couple of days?" she questioned, remembering the voice at Roseberg's practically commanding her to order strawberry ice cream.

You tell me, it suggested.

"That's not very helpful. But... thanks, I guess. My name's Winter."

I am aware. You're Winter Barnes. Friend -- or, should I say, best friend *-- to Adam Williams.*

She was perplexed by the mention of Adam's name. "How do you know that?"

No response.

"I'm not sure I understand. How do you know who I am? How do you know so much about me?"

I've been watching you and your friend.

"Adam?"

Yes. He's told his new friends all about you.

"He has?" Her voice tilted.

Indeed, he has.

Winter smiled, but it began to vanish as she looked at herself in the mirror. All she saw was a smudge. She turned around and the thing was there just as it was before, staring at her blankly. She whirled back towards the mirror, and it was a smudge. *How could this be?* she thought. *What is going on? What am I* doing *here?*

Then she remembered.

Her mom.

Her dad.

Her parents.

Her town.

Adam.

How could she have forgotten?

It was like lightning had struck in her mind. "I-I should get going. It was lovely to meet you, but I have to go," she began as she slowly but *not* surely backed away from the creature. Thing. Entity. Monster?

Its blank gaze shifted to one of worry, although she couldn't tell if it was real or fake. Its eyebrows, appearing out of nowhere, concentrated on her, gluing her to the spot. She found herself to be unable to move.

My dear Winter, why would you ever wish to leave? You have everything you could ever want.

"I'm not sure I do."

It softened, returning to its former state. *You can have anything. All you need to do is ask. Ask, and it shall be yours. Your wish is my command.*

She softened. "Really?"

Of course. Tell me anything.

"I-uh..." she found herself at a loss for words, too overwhelmed by the endless possibilities. She began to feel uneasy, her head pounding as she searched for an answer.

Something isn't quite right, she thought. *Something is missing.*

Then she remembered.

She remembered Adam.

She remembered her life in Redwick.

She remembered her family.

"I want to be reunited with my family," she declared.

It just stared at her. *Haven't you already?*

It took her a minute to get what he meant. "Oh. Yeah, I guess I have. Adam is like family to me."

See? Why leave? Your true family lies here.

Think, Winter, think, she thought to herself. There was a reason, wasn't there? It was right on the tip of her-

"Like I said, my parents. Being here is nice and all, but I want to go back. And I'm taking Adam with me before I forget anything else." She turned around, ready to leave, but she collided head-first with the monster, breaking into its ghastly threshold.

It was cold. She felt as if the life had been sucked out of her, but she was still somehow living. She felt trapped -- she *was* trapped -- inside this blurry mass of fog and horror. She'd lost all sense of direction.

Happiness didn't exist here. Every emotion twisted itself into some altered version of fear, paralyzing Winter to the core.

Within mere seconds, the terrible sensation vanished. It was almost like it had never happened.

She was alone in the bathroom.

The monster was gone.

Chapter Twelve

"Hey, Winter, you're back!" Richie shouted, waving. "You missed the entire movie!"

Amelia shushed him. "It's okay. It's showing every day. We can watch it again tomorrow."

Winter wondered what "tomorrow" would entail. What *anything* was supposed to entail.

Adam frowned. "What's wrong, Winter? You don't look so good."

"I-I'm fine," she lied.

He let out a sarcastic laugh. "No, you're not. Come with me. I know *just* the thing to cheer you up."

He gently grabbed her arm, dragging her, Amelia, and Richie along with him.

"Where are we going?" Winter asked, an edge of anticipation escaping through her voice.

"You'll see," he grinned, chipper than ever.

They flew past the movie theater in a vibrant haze, the smell of popcorn and the essence of retold stories gently fading away. It was strange how quickly everything changed. The main street whooshed by as Adam pulled her along. She glided by coffee shops, cafes, small bookstores, and even a pharmacy serving ice cream. The possibilities were endless. It was incredible how much she'd been missing out on. All along, this other Redwick had been right here. She couldn't believe how much she'd been missing.

"We're here!" Adam exclaimed, not-so-gently drifting Winter out of her daydream. "Welcome to Bentley's Diner! Richie's favorite." He nudged Richie in the side.

All of a sudden, it felt as if the universe had plucked out her desires and replaced them with untimely dread. She remembered why she'd felt any concern in the first place. This should've been Roseberg's Diner... if this was a picture-perfect world, where was her favorite diner?

"Where is Roseberg's?" Winter asked.

The three looked at her with confusion.

"What's Roseberg's?" Adam asked.

Her heart plummeted. "What do you mean? We used to go there and get ice cream together. You always got strawberry, remember?"

Adam's gaze showed no signs of recognition. "I'm sorry, but I don't know what you're talking about. Are you sure you're okay?"

She glared at him. "You know what? I've had enough of this. First, you forget how we met, then Redwick, then our seats in the theater, and now our strawberry ice cream. It's like you don't even care about our friendship anymore." Her eyes began to well up with tears, but she blinked them away.

Adam looked genuinely guilty. "Winter, I'm so sorry, but I truly have no clue what you're talking about. Maybe you have me mixed up with someone else?"

"That's it. I'm leaving. I'm going home."

"No, Winter, wait. Don't you think you're overreacting a little bit? It's horrible that you're feeling this way, but you have no reason to be mad at me. I didn't do anything wrong."

"Well, it feels like you did! Or maybe I'm the one who did something wrong. I don't know. This place..." Winter trailed off. "It's lovely. It's perfect. *Too* perfect. There's something not right about it, and I'm going to figure out what it is."

Before anyone could stop her, she ran off into the woods.

* * *

"Why doesn't anything make sense?" she shouted out loud as she desperately ran through the Redwick woodlands, searching for an explanation.

She ran for what felt like hours, tree after tree whooshing through her peripheral vision. The world flashed as she passed them, leaves becoming blobs and sticks becoming one-dimensional lines.

Exhausted, she collapsed onto a mossy bed, dangling her fingers in an adjacent stream. She ran her fingers through the water, the *unnaturally fresh* water, and closed her eyes, listening to the sounds of the flowing stream.

The calming sensation helped her feel more at ease. She still felt like something was wrong, but her fight-or-flight response had dwindled down.

After a few moments of peace and relaxation, she opened her eyes, expecting to find a familiar place, but, instead, her eyes latched onto a familiar *face*.

It was the monster.

Or maybe it wasn't.

It looked different... like it had been *disturbed*.

Its eyes were black, endless pits of despair.

She blinked.

Hello again, Winter.

"What's going on? I need answers!" Winter shouted.

Come, now, don't fret. There is nothing wrong. Everything is perfect.

"If everything is perfect, why do I feel like this?"

That's a good question. Maybe you need more. *What else do you desire, Winter? Your wish is my command.*

"I have enough, thanks. Why is everything so perfect? It's not natural."

Ah, I thought you may feel like this. You are a clever, witty individual, after all.

Winter lightened at the compliment.

You feel as though you do not deserve the specialties presented to you. But I'm here to tell you that you do. If you stay here, you will learn to love yourself and everything given to you. It's important to be grateful, after all.

Winter felt her heart drop. Something wasn't right, and she'd known it for a while. She knew what she had to do.

"Thank you for the hospitality and for everything nice you have provided me. I appreciate it. Especially the movie theater. But-"

Do you really *want to return to an empty, abandoned movie theater? Or parents who don't care about your loss? Or, worse, a world without your best friend?* She stiffened. *Adam is here, and he always will be. He has chosen to stay rather than leave. Don't you want to be with him forever?*

"Yeah, but-"

Then why leave? Adam may not be happy with you if you do.

Oh... she hadn't thought about that. "I guess that would be selfish. But isn't leaving my parents also selfish?"

The monster shook its head. *It's not selfish. They simply don't care about you as I do -- I mean, as we do.*

Did it just say "I," as if it cared more about her than Adam did? More than her friends?

"No. I've made my decision. I'm leaving. I appreciate everything you've done for me, and so does everyone else. But I'm leaving. And they're coming with me."

The monster let out a distorted-sounding screech, curling in on itself in wretched anger. Instead of the smudgy mass of black and white it had been before, it became an aggressive bunch of lines, as if someone had grabbed the nearest pencil and scribbled all of their negative feelings out onto paper -- only it was real. Winter shrieked.

Do you really think you can just leave? *You selfish, foolish girl. Why would you want to leave your friends? They won't come with you. You'll be all alone.*

"No, I won't. I'll never be alone again, now that I know Adam is alive. And now that I have Amelia and Richie. You can't destroy friendship -- you're not even a part of it. And why are you being so mean?"

It let out another shriek, causing Winter to wimp. *I have done everything for you, and you appreciate none of it.*

"I do! I said so!"

The monster laughed, reverberating the forest around her. She lost her balance, falling flat on the ground.

You think you're so smart, that you've figured out my game – but your word means nothing! You're a selfish, ungrateful little girl. You can leave if you wish, but you are not taking Adam or anyone else with you.

"Why not? Why do you want them to stay here so badly?"

Because I love them. You should learn a thing or two about love, you know.

Winter teared up. "Love? Is this what you call loving someone? Manipulating them into staying with you by giving them what they want? No. That's not love. Love is true devotion. Love is wanting the best for someone no matter what you wish they would do instead. Love is supporting them through tough times. You'll never understand true friendship. I'm out of here."

She ran off, her tears creating a waterfall on the ground.

Chapter Thirteen

She ran and ran and ran until her feet were covered in blisters. She continued until she found her friends, who were patiently waiting outside the movie theater.

"Hey! Where'd you run off to?" Richie asked.

"Winter, you look awful! What happened?" Amelia asked.

Adam ran up to her. "Are you okay?"

To answer all of their questions, she said, "No. I'm not okay. And you aren't either. Something is going on here, and we need to leave. Right now."

They all looked puzzled.

"Why would we leave?" Richie questioned. "We have everything!"

"Yeah, why do you want to leave?" Amelia asked.

She paused, momentarily uncertain of herself. She then had a terrible realization. *That's what it wants you to think,* she thought to herself. *To feel unsure of yourself. To doubt yourself.* "Don't you guys realize that something is going on here? Something bad?"

They all looked at her as if she'd sprouted another arm.

"Nothing here is bad, Winter. Everything is fine- I mean, perfect. Sooo perfect." Adam awkwardly stared at his shoes.

Winter wasn't convinced. She knew Adam well enough to know when he was lying. She looked at him suspiciously, sure that he was up to something.

Adam looked back, equally suspicious. *What?* His eyes said (of course, his eyes didn't *really* talk. They were like twins, in a sense. They communicated through a sort of telepathy. Again, she highly doubted they were *actually* telepathic as she knew he was keeping a secret and she couldn't decipher it.)

You know what, her eyes retorted. *You're acting weird.*

He looked at her a moment longer, then looked away, ignoring her.

Fine. Be that way, she communicated.

Winter took a step towards him. "Adam, I need to speak with you in private."

Richie and Amelia exchanged a look, clearly confused as to why they were being left out.

"Anything you can say to me you can say to Richie and Amelia." He gestured to the two.

Winter crossed her arms. "No, I can't. Sorry. I trust you guys, I really do. It's just something I need to speak with Adam about alone," she said.

"It's alright. We understand," Amelia said sadly.

"Come on, Amelia, let's go do something together. Just us. Without *them*. They don't care about us anyway," Richie declared with distaste. He and Amelia walked away, leaving Adam and Winter alone.

"What's this about?" Adam asked, his tone accusatory.

"Why are you acting like this?"

"Like what?"

"You *know* what. You're hiding something."

Adam shifted uneasily. "N-no I'm not. Why would I have anything to hide?"

"That's exactly what I'm wondering."

"What makes you think I'm hiding something?"

"I know that you've been lying to me. You don't actually think this place is perfect. Why do you pretend that it is?"

Adam exhaled. "Listen, Winter, I'm not supposed to tell you."

That piqued her interest. "Tell me what...?"

"Nothing! Like I said, this place is perfect. It's the best place in the world." He forced a smile, but his eyes told her otherwise.

"I'm not convinced. You can tell me, Adam, really. You can trust me."

His eyes saddened. "You think I don't trust you?"

Winter shook her head, guilty for implying that she had thought so. "No! I know that you do. I just don't understand why you won't tell me."

"I'm sorry. I truly am. I really can't tell you."

Winter's suspicion grew. Something deeply unsettling was going on. She turned, preparing to walk away.

Adam ran in front of her. "What are you doing?"

"I'm going to find out what you're hiding from me. If you won't tell me, I'll find out myself."

Adam continued to block her way. "No! Trust me, you don't want to know." He looked around, then lowered his voice to a near whisper. "Listen to me. I didn't want to say anything because I was scared I would hurt you, but I think it's too late for that. You're already in too deep and you deserve to know what's going on. I will tell you. But it has to be somewhere hidden. Somewhere it won't listen."

"Who?"

"I can't tell you. Not here. We need to go somewhere else."

"Why not here?"

Adam sighed. "Winter, I'm sorry, we're in a rush. Please slow down with the questions."

Winter felt a little hurt, but she understood. "Okay. Let's go."

Adam held out his hand, waiting for her to take it. The moment she took it, he ran off, pulling her along with him. She had absolutely no idea where he was taking her. Confused, she kept up her pace to match his.

Eventually, he led her to a familiar clearing. The exit to the maze. Where she'd left one world and entered another.

Adam raised his pointer finger to his lip and mimicked a *shush*ing sound. He beckoned her along into the tunnel.

"I don't understand. Why are we here?"

Adam sighed. "Alright. We're safe now. It can't spy on us here."

"How so?"

"Once we enter the mirror maze, we're out of its grasp. It can't take any more of ourselves away. It all comes rushing back to you. The memories of home, its twisted lies -- all of it."

"But I feel the same."

"That's because you're different. You care about people, Winter, and you refused to let that go. You held onto your willpower, which it wasn't prepared for. I had completely lost all will to fight back and leave. When I wandered into this tunnel, all of my memories came back to me. I felt like myself again. I knew I had to get out, but I couldn't leave Amelia and Richie here. And I can't just leave it here. It could grab any innocent child and take their future away. Take their lives away."

Winter frowned. "Who are you referring to?"

Adam tensed. That was when Winter realized who -- or rather, what -- he meant.

"Do you hear it, too?" she asked, worried that she was crazy and he would either dismiss her or have no idea what she was talking about.

But she knew he wouldn't do that to her.

Adam looked at her. *Really* looked at her. She stared into his caramel eyes. "Yes. We all do."

That got her attention. "We? You mean Richie and Amelia?"

"We're trapped here, Winter. Every one of us. We all had lives before here, lives we weren't satisfied with enough to stay. The story is the same for all of us." He paused, taking a deep breath. "It started with the whispering. We were bored with our lives, so we listened to it. We ignored any initial gut instinct that warned us against stranger danger. We all started hearing the whispering a couple of days before the carnival opened. When we got to the carnival, we were drawn to one particular attraction: the mirror maze. As soon as we found it, we went inside, led along by the whispering."

Winter stilled. "All of this-"

"Happened to you, too. I know. But I'm here to warn you. Nothing about this is okay. Curiosity got the best of us. It's been who knows how long and none of us – neither Amelia nor Richie and soon me, too – remember how we got here. But I do. I remember. I remember everything."

Winter froze. Something was still out of place. "But you don't always remember. Maybe you do now, but sometimes you forget."

Adam nodded solemnly. "Yes. Sometimes I do. That's how it works. It – the whispering -- it gets into your head. It convinces you that everything is perfect. None of us are oblivious, Winter. We all suspected something was going on. When we wanted to leave, it visited us and convinced us not to. We fell prey to its false promises." He sighed. "We were all terrified. But I refused to let go of my past. To let go of you. I knew that the clock was ticking and I would soon forget everything, too. So, I made a plan: to lie my way out. When it confronted me, also in the movie theater bathroom, right after I'd left 2B--" Winter brightened at this, touched and a little bit relieved that he remembered their movie theater traditions – "I pretended everything was fine. Not just fine: perfect. I told it that it was right and that I would stay. That I believed everything to be perfect. It's just... I made one mistake. One mistake I'll never be able to take back." He began to tear up.

Winter held his hand. "What's wrong? No matter what you did, it couldn't have been that bad."

Adam was full-on crying. "That's it. That's the problem. You're here. You wouldn't be here if it weren't for me." He sniffed.

"What do you mean?"

He briefly closed his eyes, tears streaking down his face. "I told it that... that something was missing."

"Missing from what?"

"From this world. In order for it to be 'perfect,' I needed you. You're my best friend, Winter. I didn't realize it was going to take you, too. But I still betrayed you." Despite his efforts to cover up his tears, a wayward tear splashed onto the floor. She joined him, crying at the unfairness of it all.

Winter placed her hands on his shoulders. "Adam, listen to me. You didn't betray me. You're the best friend I've ever had. I'm just glad you remembered me."

"How could I forget you? Friendships can be tough, and they don't always last, but sometimes they can be everlasting. And I know without a doubt that ours is one of those. A forever friendship."

Winter smiled despite the tears. "You're the best friend anyone could ever ask for, Adam." She hugged him, the hug so comforting and warm that she never wanted to let go.

She reluctantly released her hold on him. "But I still don't get why you feel like you betrayed me. All you did was say my name."

Adam's gaze shifted downwards. "Whenever I mention something or someone I'm longing to have or see, it listens. It obeys, bringing us whatever delights we desire. So, it sought you out and brought you here. I realized too late what I had said -- what I'd done to you. I'm so sorry."

Winter placed her hand on his shoulder. "Adam. You didn't do anything wrong. All you wanted was to not be alone. No one deserves to be in a situation like this. We're together now. That's what matters. I'm here, and I'm going to help you fight this monster. We're going to free everyone stuck here – Richie, Amelia, and anyone else. We will get out of this."

Adam was still crying, only these were tears of relief. "Promise?"

"I promise."

Chapter Fourteen

Winter and Adam finally located Amelia and Richie.

"What do you want?" Richie asked harshly.

Amelia looked down, manners aside. Winter felt a twinge of guilt for making her and Richie feel left out.

"I'm disappointed in you both," Amelia said curtly. "You acted very immaturely, excluding us like that. We're friends. We're meant to stick together."

Winter's guilt intensified, remembering her earlier promise to Adam. She'd vowed to stick with him and help him, Amelia, and Richie get out of this. Through friendship. Had she really made Amelia and Richie feel as though their friendship didn't mean anything to her?

"I'm so sorry I made you feel that way. You two – you *three* – are the best friends I've ever had." Amelia's mouth pointed upwards in the beginning of a smile. Richie, still hesitant, looked at his shoes, kicking a stone. "Friendship is everything to me. I was so preoccupied with rekindling my friendship with Adam that I didn't pay much attention to you guys. I'm sorry. I will do better, I promise. I really mean it."

This won Amelia's full smile. "It's okay. We understand. I'm so happy we're friends." She gave Winter a warm hug.

Richie was harder to convince. "How do we know you won't break that promise?"

Winter looked at him. "I never break a promise. The only way I would be is if I died, which I'm hoping won't happen anytime soon. But even through death, I will stick by you. I'll always be with you."

Richie broke into a grin. "Thanks, Winter. You're the best." He brought her into a warm embrace.

Adam hugged Amelia. "Are we all hugging now?" she said, laughing.

The four of them laughed until their stomachs hurt. It was a good feeling.

Reality settled in. Winter's smile vanished. "We need to go to the mirror maze."

The mere mention of the maze brought shock upon Amelia and Richie's faces, neither of them expecting Winter to mention this secret they'd been concealing.

"You hear it too?" Amelia asked.

Winter nodded. "Yes. We all do. And we're going to stop it."

Adam gasped. "Winter!" he hissed through his teeth. "You're not supposed to say that out in the open!"

Winter, realizing the crucial mistake she'd made, put her hand to her mouth. *Maybe it'll be okay?* she thought.

But it wasn't.

The sky rumbled, turning from a crystal-clear blue to an ominous foreboding charcoal gray. The sun was swallowed by the clouds.

"Oh no. I've ruined it. I'm so sorry." Tears streamed down Winter's face.

Amelia placed a hand on her shoulder. "Winter, everybody makes mistakes. It's only natural. It will be alright. We will still get out of this. We just have to stick together."

Winter sniffed. "You're right. We'll get through this if we stick together."

Adam and Richie came closer and the four of them shared a brief yet powerful embrace, one of the first they'd shared together, and possibly the last.

It began to pour.

Not rain.

Hail.

"Ouch!" Amelia yelped. It only hailed harder.

Winter Barnes, a familiar voice declared.

Winter gasped.

This time, it wasn't a whisper.

It was a growl. A threatening one.

"Do you guys hear that?"

Everyone nodded. "Yes."

The sky boomed. Thunder rumbled. There was a harsh strike of lightning, revealing the hideous monster.

It reminded Winter of a nightmare; one where everything was desolate and bleak. She felt as if she would never be warm again. The thought chilled her to her bones, bringing on a shiver when she realized how real it was. She was horrified.

You dare think you can outsmart me? Hah! You slipped up like I knew you would. I had no faith in you. Neither did your friends.

That hurt.

Adam shook his head. "That's not true. It's trying to mess with your mind."

Richie nodded. "It got in my head, too. I still remember my brother."

Winter looked at him. "You remember him?"

"Of course I do. I may have forgotten most things, but I'll never forget him. He's my brother. My best friend. Besides you guys, obviously. Don't worry, you aren't replacements or anything. Just additions!"

That got a brief laugh from everyone.

They're lying to you, Winter.

Its growl had lowered to a whisper.

Her friends all looked happy. She wondered if they hadn't heard it. With a bone-rattling chill, Winter realized that it was only speaking to her, and her alone.

They don't love you. They aren't your real friends. They don't care about your happiness. They want you to stay with them forever. They're keeping you from going home to your parents.

"What do you want? One minute you want me to stay, one you want me to go."

Her friends looked confused.

"Is it talking to you?" Amelia asked carefully.

Winter nodded.

You can do whatever you please. Don't you want to stay here forever, Winter? Why go back to a family who doesn't care about your friendship? You can stay here with Adam. Amelia and Richie will go back home.

"But I want everyone to go back home."

As you wish. But it comes at a price.

"I don't care. I'll pay the price. I'll do anything for my friends."

You stay here with me. Forever.

Winter's heart felt like it stopped beating. "Stay... here?"

Everyone's eyes widened.

Forever.

"And if I do this, my friends will be safe? They'll go back home?"

"No, Winter, don't do this!" Adam called out.

Amelia nodded. "Don't stay here."

"You don't have to do this," Richie said.

Winter shook her head. "Yes, I do. If I don't, I'm not keeping my promise. I really don't care what happens to me as long as you all are okay."

Adam shook his head. "I can't be happy knowing you're stuck here. Honestly." He turned to face the monster. "Keep both of us. Set Amelia and Richie free."

"Adam, no!" Winter called out, but it was too late.

The monster's face contorted into a twisted smile. It wasn't a happy smile. It looked smug... like it was satisfied. Game over. It had gotten what it wanted. It had won.

"No!" Amelia and Richie shouted out at the same time.

"Take us, too!" Amelia declared. Richie looked appalled, then nodded, silently pledging his loyalty.

No. You two are no longer of any use to me. I have minimal usage left out of this one – it turned to Richie, who frowned – *but none from this one.* He turned to Amelia.

"What do you mean?" asked Amelia.

Amelia Sunbury, do you remember anything about your old life?

Amelia creased her brows, thinking hard. "Um... yeah. Of course I do. I remember..." She stood still, speechless. Her shoulders dropped. "Oh. I guess I really don't."

Exactly. Now you are mine.

"What? No, I'm not."

Lightning struck as its anger intensified. *Yes, you are. You've lost your roots. You remember nothing about your old life. After all, who are you if you don't remember your past?*

"The past isn't important," Amelia declared. "What matters is the present, and how you decide to act going forward."

That stuck with Winter. Up until recently, she'd lived her life dwelling on the past, unwilling to move on and focus on the present. Now she knew how important it was to live in the moment and appreciate what she had.

"Your tricks don't faze us," Richie said.

"And you're forgetting one thing," Adam chimed in. "It doesn't steal our values. And the new memories and friendships we make along the way."

But what about Winter? You don't even remember how you became friends.

Winter's esteem and confidence deflated. "Oh right. You don't remember, do you?"

Adam shifted his gaze to the ground. His eyes began to fill with tears. "No... I don't. I'm so sorry," his voice wobbled. "I'm a terrible friend."

"Don't say that. Adam, you're the best friend I could ever have." Feeling guilty, she looked at Amelia and Richie. "Don't worry, I love you guys, too, but I haven't gotten to know you as well as I know Adam." Together, the four of them shared a smile.

"Thank you, Winter," Adam said. "But am I really a good friend if I don't remember how we met? If I don't remember much about our friendship before I arrived here?"

"Adam, listen to me. It's out of your control. It isn't your fault that you don't remember that." She paused. "You know whose fault it is?

Do you know who *stole* your memories from you?" She turned to the monster.

It turned towards her.

Be careful where you tread, Winter Barnes. It would be better if you didn't disrespect me. You don't want to get on my bad side. I'm quite tricky to displease.

She scoffed. "You've sentenced Adam and me to stay here forever. I think we're already on your bad side."

"Yeah, we hate you," Richie said. Amelia nodded in agreement, knowing that "hate" was a vulgar word, but she nonetheless put her opinion in that word.

"You're a terrible, terrible thing," Adam spat out. "You have no right to take away our freedom."

Then, a terrible, terrible thing happened.

The monster contorted itself into a figure so indistinguishable that Winter was not sure if it was the same creature she'd seen before. Its eyes were hollow, leaking oozing, black liquid from its sockets. Its smile twisted into a chilling, demonic grin, spooking Winter soulless.

Everyone was frightened out of their wits.

I told you not to disrespect me. I was going to give you four more time, but I've decided your time is up.

Winter looked at her friends in horror. *No,* Winter thought. *This can't be happening.*

Without further hesitation, the world around them started to twist and turn. All color leaked out of the world, turning black and white like an old film. The grass narrowed, the water evaporated, and the ground rumbled. The earth began to shake and fall apart, taking every living thing with it. Winter gradually noticed everything and everyone around her begin to fade.

First, Amelia started to disappear.

Amelia, who had forgotten -- no, lost -- every last bit of her past faded slowly at first but faded faster and faster as she had less and less to lose. She was nearly the opposite of opaque. Before Winter knew it, she was gone, and there was nothing she could do.

She couldn't even scream.

Then, Richie.

She watched Richie, the longest resident of the monster's world, become increasingly more and more transparent. He faded into the abyss, visibly lost to all creation.

Finally, Adam, her closest friend, fell victim to the monster's curse, slowly fading; but he refused to fall into the monster's grasp. He fought and fought, ebbing between near opacity and transparency, unwilling to let go.

"You won't catch me! I'll never forget. I'll never forget my best friend," Adam shouted through choking sobs.

Too late, the monster warned.

Adam's unsteady opacity faded in and out like a spark of electricity. He held on. "No. I'll never be yours. You won't take me."

Maybe I don't have you just yet, the monster growled, its eyes never-ending pits of despair and turmoil. *But I have sweet, lovely Amelia. Such a shame she'll never live up to her full potential. And dashing, brazen Richie. He charmed the lives of those he loved, humoring them when they needed it most. And now he's gone.*

"You had no right," Winter said gravely. "Amelia and Richie were wonderful, beautiful people. They were loyal to the very last second of their lives, and I'm proud to call them my friends."

Come, now, Winter. Why the long face? You still have your best friend right here. Why dwell upon your other friends? It gestured to Adam, his form trembling.

Winter grimaced. "You disgust me. Just because they weren't my *best* friends doesn't make their losses hurt any less. And I'm confident to say they would've both become my best friends had we had more time together. We're all immune to your little tricks. All four of us are unstoppable, and you know it. I refuse to let you ruin any more lives. Now, go!"

As you wish, the monster said. And, with that, it vanished without a trace.

Winter waited a few moments just to make sure she and Adam were safe. "We did it," she breathed. "We saved ourselves."

"What makes you so sure?" Adam said, breaking his silence. He glared at her. "You're just a lonely, selfish little brat. Just let it go."

Winter stared at him, betrayed. "Adam, why would you say that?"

"Because I'm the only one who truly cares for you. Leave everyone behind and stay here with me. Forever. No monster, just me. Your best friend."

She frowned. "If you truly cared for me, you wouldn't say such things."

"Now look who's doubting our friendship. Gee, Winter, you really are the stupid little girl everyone thinks you are. Don't you see? I'm willing to stick by your side forever. That's what a best friend does. Now, will you stay with me or not?"

Winter considered his offer. Was she really just a selfish, lonely little girl? Did she not understand what true friendship was supposed to be? Was she a bad friend?

Then it hit her. "No. I won't stay with you, because you're a bad friend. You're not Adam."

Adam glared at her, the hatred in his eyes so unfamiliar yet recognizable. "I think you need to reconsider who is the bad friend here. You're the one shouting accusations at me. How do you think that makes me feel?"

Winter believed none of it. "Adam would never say that. The Adam I know is loyal. He's considerate. He would never say something like that. That's how I know you aren't him. You're the monster. You've taken over his body, but you can't control his mind. You may be clever, but I won't let you trick me."

Adam -- the monster -- faltered. "You foolish, impotent girl! You may have figured me out, but your words can't outsmart me!"

Winter shook her head. "My words can't, but my beliefs will. I believe that you have trapped children here for too long, and I'm here to put a stop to it. I'll do anything, even if it means sacrificing myself."

Monster-Adam tilted his head. She'd piqued his interest.

"Do you give your word?"

"My word for what?"

"That you'll stay here with me. Forever. No matter what."

"Only if you set everyone free. Let Amelia and Richie rest in peace. Let Adam go."

"He won't be with you," monster-Adam sneered.

"I care more about his freedom and peace than about my being with him. I want you to set him free."

Monster-Adam considered. "Fine. I will let Amelia and Richie go. Adam will go peacefully. And you will stay with me forever. Do you promise?"

Winter readied herself. "Yes. I promise that I'll stay here with you... forever. No matter what."

Monster-Adam smiled. It pained Winter to see the monster taking control of Adam's sweet, happy looks. They didn't belong together.

"Good." And, with that, the monster left Adam's body.

Moments passed before Adam -- the real Adam -- awoke with a start, coughing relentlessly.

"Adam!" Winter, already by his side, put her hands out to steady him as he stood.

"That wasn't me. I didn't mean any of those things I said. You have to believe me."

"Adam, of course I believe you. I know that you would never act like that. You're too kind, loyal, and thoughtful to say such things."

Adam smiled. "Thank you, Winter. That means a lot to me." Then he collapsed as he rapidly began to fade from the world.

Winter knelt as she reached out to touch him, her hand almost passing through. "No, not now. You don't deserve this." She'd been sobbing before, but these tears were gentle, slow. She'd known this was coming, but that didn't take away from her pain. It was too great to be conveyed in an action as common as crying. Her eyes were empty. She could barely cry at all.

"I know this is hard to hear, but sometimes, bad things happen, no matter how hard we try to prevent them. The good thing is I'm about to be set free. My only regret is that you aren't, too. But I believe in you. You will defeat this monster, and you will get out of here, one way or another. Just know that Amelia, Richie, and I will be with you the whole time."

"I-I know. I love you, Adam. I just wish I'd gotten to tell Amelia and Richie that."

"You didn't have to say it. They already know." His voice became quieter and quieter, soon to be lost.

"I'm going to take down that monster. For Amelia. For Richie. For you."

Adam smiled. "You always were fond of justice." Like the flick of a switch, he vanished.

Grief was too simple a word to explain how she felt. She felt as if her soul had been ripped out and consumed by the monster. She screamed, trying to drown out the unfairness of it all. After what felt like hours, the screaming stopped, and she collapsed, watching the monster come closer and closer into view. It was time.

Despite everything, she smiled. She'd gotten what she'd wished for. Amelia and Richie were safe, and so was Adam. They were free.

Chapter Fifteen

Now it's time for your end of the bargain. You're going to stay here with me. Forever.

Winter mustered up as much nonchalance as possible. "I guess that's only fair. How does this work? Do I disappear, too?"

The monster frowned, its eyebrows concaving into sharp, brutal arrows. *What's this? Sarcasm? Playing pretend? Don't act like this doesn't affect you, Winter. You wouldn't dare make me angrier than I already am.*

Winter shrugged. "Guess what? I *dare*."

It smiled that awful grin of its, contorting itself into the most twisted of contortions, not stopping until a slight glimmer of fear shone its way through Winter's eyes, impossible for her to resist. She trembled under the bloody, malevolent gaze of the monster, unable to keep her nonchalant guise up.

You're not so smug after all. Now look who's scared?

Winter laughed. She actually *laughed*. Despite the severity of the situation, and her knowing the immense and life-threatening pressure she was under, she was amused as she looked the obvious solution right in the eye. "You know what? I'm done here. I think this whole time I've had the choice to just leave, and you've been distracting me from making that choice. Well, I choose it now. I'm out of here. Good riddance, you filthy, abominable monster."

And, with that, she ran.

She ran for her life.

She ran for her family.

She ran for her friends.
She ran for her home.

Chapter Sixteen

Winter ran and ran and ran until her legs were moving on autopilot.

She had to focus.

She had one destination: the mirror maze.

And the monster was *not* going to prevent her from leaving.

It couldn't, it *wouldn't*, take anything else from her. Not this time.

You'll regret it, the jeering voice hissed, the tone echoing through her ears and later finding its way into her nightmares.

She ignored it, unwilling to be distracted from the task at hand.

She had to get home.

This was her only shot.

She whooshed past Bentley's, the false stand-in for her beloved Roseberg's Diner. Oh, how she missed Mrs. Roseberg --*Whoops! I meant Minnie,* she thought with a smile. She wouldn't take another thing for granted again.

Don't you dare ignore me.

I'm all you have. All you've ever had.

It'll only worsen things if you leave.

You have no one.

You're all alone.

No matter how much it hurt, she pushed away the empty threats, staying true to her strong beliefs that she *did* have someone. She had Adam, Amelia, and Richie, even if they weren't alive anymore. She wondered if they'd stopped being alive a long time ago, their lives lost to the deep depths of the monster's bottomless craving for innocent souls to keep. But Winter had a chance at freedom. She would get out of this. She would do this for Adam. For Amelia. For Richie. For her friends.

She panted relentlessly, sheer willpower the sole motivator for her to keep up with herself. She flew past the theater, her and Adam's beloved theater, ever so briefly basking in the old memories they'd made there and soaking up the new ones to take with her, into her dreams.

It felt like hours before she finally reached the mirror maze, the monster still on her trail. She wouldn't let it get to her, not this time.

It was gaining on her. She had to run faster. She tried and tried, but her body couldn't keep up with her. She collapsed onto the dirt-strewn ground, limbs sprawled about like she was a dying bug, exhausted beyond relief. Before she could even grasp what was happening, the monster engulfed her, surrounding her with the dreary, isolating fog she was all too familiar with.

Winter was hopelessly enveloped in a cold, desolate embrace. In here, wherever *here* was, time slowed, or, at least, it seemed to. Her emotions twisted and turned, allowing the monster to absorb her happiness and sense of belonging, snatching her willpower away in a single grasp.

Any desire to fight back vanquished immediately; what reason did she have to fight, anyway? She was trapped. She would always be alone.

The last time she was trapped here, she got out. This time was different. She would never escape. She would never get out.

It had finally won.

"No," she admitted in defeat.

It's too late, Winter. You're mine.

"I refuse to let you do this."

The monster let out a haughty, smug laugh, echoing deep within its miserable chambers, shaking Winter until she was unbearably dizzy. She closed her eyes, unwilling to accept this evil she had been trapped in.

Your childish beliefs amuse me. Stop trying. It's over. There's nothing you can do.

"Stop," she begged, her voice rapidly fading to a whisper. She relented. Why was she trying so hard to get out? There was nothing she could do. And why did she want to leave so urgently, anyway? There must've been a reason… there must have been…

She fell to the ground, on the edge of consciousness. The ringing in her ears was enough to block out the noise of the monster. She closed her eyes, waiting for the monster to fully take her in. She would get it over with, she reasoned with herself. Like ripping off a Band-Aid.

Any last words?

"You're cruel," she uttered.

The world around her trembled like an earthquake. *I will not tolerate this any longer. You're mistaken. I've offered you everything you could ever want. Your friends are at peace. At least be grateful for that before I take you.*

Something it said sounded familiar. Something…

Winter opened her eyes, realizing the mistake the monster had made. It had let something slip.

Her friends.

The people she loved.

She remembered why she was here.

And why she had to get out.

"No," she said. "You won't take me."

And, with that declaration, she slammed into the edge of her trap, ready to escape.

She fought and fought against the monster's threshold. *You can't leave. You're staying with me. You promised. And you would never* dare *break a promise.*

"See, the funny thing about promises is that I only make them with people I trust. I trust Adam. I trust Amelia. I trust Richie. I trust my family. I most certainly do not trust *you*." She felt a twinge of guilt for blocking out her family. Her mother, who only wanted what was best for her. Her father, who knew just what to do when she wasn't feeling her best. She winced, wishing she'd fulfilled her promise as a loyal daughter. She would make it up to them.

With this, she pushed and pushed and *pushed*. The monster hesitated, its threshold weakening. It wasn't much, but it was a start.

"No matter how much you try and stop me, I will leave here. I will put an end to this." Her certainty echoed across the monster's trap, further weakening its hold on her.

If you leave here, are you really going to be happy? Your friends are dead. *You're all alone. You have nobody to go back to.*

"That's where you're wrong." Its hold on her continued to weaken. She could almost push through to the other side. "I have my parents. I have people who love me. I still love them, even if they're gone. They will always be with me. I will always have their love. That's something you can never take away from me."

The monster's threshold flickered, its visibility decreasing by the minute.

Stay with me. I can bring your friends back. I can bring back everyone.

"Even if you can, they're resting. I would not dare disturb them and subject them to be with you. Leave them be. Leave everyone be. Just let go."

It let out a piercing shriek. It didn't faze her. "You've tormented innocent people for too long. I don't even know *why* you do this, why you steal children away for your own satisfaction, but it's over. Everything you've ever done is over."

She fell to the ground. The monster was nowhere in sight.

It was gone. It had to be.

She knew what she had to do. Without further hesitation, she searched for the mirror maze.

She approached the abandoned carnival, searching for the mirror maze. She flew past the merry-go-round, the echoes of dying laughter drifting over her head as she recognized how fake it all was.

Winter stopped, out of breath. She put her hands to her knees, heaving.

She took a moment to catch her breath before continuing her search. After passing an abandoned ticket booth and some terrifyingly tall ride that she would never dare go on, she finally located the mirror maze.

It grew closer and closer as she ran, losing all feeling in her legs. She powered through, reaching the entrance.

As she moved to walk inside, a familiar voice froze her to the ground. *Winter Barnes.*

"You. You're still here."

Barely. I'm fading away.

Its voice was lower than the quietest whisper. She had to listen closely, blocking out the songs of birds and the carnival music. She wondered if she'd miss this world, but she knew it was all a ruse. She knew it was all fake.

If you ignore me, you're worse than I ever was.

She stopped.

I'm giving you one last chance. My days are over. I'm fading away. It's time for someone else to rule this world. I believe that person to be you, Winter. Stay here. Look after me. Make this world what it once was. Bring back your friends and live here with them forever. That's what you want, isn't it? Or do your loyalties lie elsewhere?

She scoffed. "Over my dead body."

With that, the whispering disappeared, and the world began to fade away.

Without a second thought, she ran into the mirror maze, leaving all her troubles behind her.

It was a tricky, cunning maze. Just when she thought she'd reached the other side, it was a dead end. When she thought she'd reached a dead end, the path continued.

Winter heard the distant sound of glass breaking. She ignored it, but it happened again and again. And it got closer and closer.

With an earth-shattering scream, she realized once the other world faded away, there would be no need for a path in between worlds. Soon, the mirror maze would cease to exist, and it could very well take her along with it.

Her chest tightened. No... this couldn't be happening. Not when she'd gotten this far.

She couldn't do this alone.

Winter squeezed her eyes shut, focusing solely on her broken heart. She thought deeply of the people she loved, the ones she was fighting for.

She opened her eyes, her gaze landing on a glowing Adam-shaped figure that had manifested in the mirror. She looked behind her, but nobody was there.

"Adam? Is that you?" Three mirrors down, there was an explosion. Glass hurled itself everywhere. Winter curled in on herself, bracing herself from the glass.

The Adam-shaped figure didn't make a sound. He nodded.

"It *is* you," she whispered, awestruck.

Adam gestured for her to follow him. "Where are you taking me?" Winter asked.

Home, a voice uttered. Her heart skipped a beat, terrified that the monster was back, that it would drag her down into the endless hole of nothing. She realized that the voice had come from Adam.

Adam led her further, then stopped. She looked up, spotting the end of the maze.

She reached out to take his hand, but it was no use. She looked into the mirror, searching for her best friend, but only found a reflection of herself. Adam wasn't there, not really. Maybe he had never been there. Maybe she'd imagined it all. Or, maybe, he was helping her one last time before he faded away. Whatever the reason, it didn't matter. She was a few footsteps away from safety, and he was somehow here with her.

One by one, the remaining mirrors began to crack.

It was now or never.

As the last mirror exploded, she ran up to the exit, jumping through and tumbling out the other side. Had she waited a moment longer, she would have been lost to the dark, endless abyss.

Winter spread her arms out to balance herself. She studied her surroundings, first recognizing the familiar Redwick carnival sights. She watched as kids rode the merry-go-round, giggling in delight as their parents snapped photos for their family photo albums. Her gaze shifted up to the impossibly tall Twister, the screams of overzealous kids regretting their decision to ride it echoing across the clearing.

She recognized the food court, spotting her anxious-looking parents along with it.

She ran towards them, waving. "MOM! DAD!" Their eyes opened in delight as they took in Winter, bruised and disheveled, covered in dirt and dust from head to toe, fresh blood trickling down her knees.

They welcomed her in for a desperate embrace. She had never felt so safe.

"Winter!" She squeezed harder, blocking Winter's airways, but she didn't mind. Her mom pulled away. "What happened to you?" her mom asked. "Are you alright?"

Winter nodded. "Yeah, I'm fine. Just got lost in the mirror maze."

"What mirror maze?" her mom asked. She shrugged, brushing it off. "We're just glad you're okay."

Her dad, beaming, lifted Winter off the ground and spun her in a circle. Before, she would've been annoyed that he was treating her this way, that she was "too old" for such things; but now, she couldn't have been more grateful.

"You have some explaining to do," her dad said. "You didn't join the circus, did you?"

Her mom jokingly slapped him. "David!" But she couldn't hide her smile. "Don't go running off again, you hear me? You're grounded for a week. You're not in trouble. We just want to keep an eye on you and make sure you're safe."

Little did she know that Winter was perfectly fine with being confined to her own home for a week.

"Come on, kiddo, let's get you home."

"Wait," she started. "There's one more thing I have to do."

"What's that?" her dad asked.

"There's someone I need to see."

* * *

Winter ran breathlessly over to Roseberg's Diner, where she knew he would be. She saw him sitting outside, reading a newspaper. He looked up as she walked over to him.

"Did you find what you were looking for?" Mr. Charleston asked.

"I sure did."

Mr. Charleston smiled. "I'm glad." He went back to reading his newspaper.

"Wait."

He looked up from his paper. "Yes?"

"It was you, wasn't it? You're the one who put up the flier?"

"I have no idea what you're talking about."

"But it had to be you. You're the only one who believed me."

"For all you know, it could've been Minnie Roseberg."

Winter shook her head. "Possibly. But I have a feeling it was you. You knew I'd see it when you told me to go to the library archives, didn't you? You wanted me to look for the mirror maze."

"I haven't the slightest idea what you are referring to. Now, if you'll excuse me," he said, looking back down at his paper.

"But-" she relented. "Alright. Have a nice afternoon, Mr. Charleston."

She detected a smile blooming across his face.

* * *

Winter lay tucked in bed with her parents sitting beside her. So what if she was thirteen? There was nothing shameful about showing your love for your family.

"Sweet dreams," her mom said, kissing her forehead.

"Goodnight, sleep tight, don't let the bed bugs bite!" Her dad jokingly opened his mouth, pretending to bite Winter. Her mom laughed to herself.

They stood up to leave.

"Wait," Winter muttered.

They turned to look back at her.

"I have something to say."

"Of course, dear, anything," her mom said, holding her hand.

She stood up, taking a deep breath. "I-I'm ready to admit it."

Her parents shared a hopeful look. "Admit what?" her mom asked. But they already knew.

"Adam. That he's gone."

"Oh, sweetie." Her parents hugged her again, and it was magically greater than the last. It was warm and welcoming, just as she needed.

"This doesn't mean I don't still love him. He was my best friend. He'll always be with me."

Her mom shed a tear. "We've never been more proud of you, honey."

Her dad ruffled her hair. "You're a great kid, you know that? We couldn't have raised a better daughter."

Winter laughed, a sound so unfamiliar to her parents that they looked at each other in surprise. She knew it would take a long time to heal. Grieving was a slow, painful process, but it was necessary. As she said, her love for her friends would always be there. Death could never sever the bond she shared with Adam, Amelia, and Richie. They would look out for her, and her for them. With that comforting thought, she closed her eyes and entered into a deep, well-deserved slumber.

Epilogue

Winter squeezed her eyes shut, attempting to block out the blazing sun. It was nearing autumn, but that didn't mean summer was over. Summer in Redwick was unlike any other; some days were boiling while others were chilly. This particular day was a chilly one; she put her hands up in the air to combat the 60º weather. The heat from the sun brought warmth and comfort to her cold fingertips.

It was the first day of school. Winter waited in anticipation at the bus stop, looking around for a familiar face that she knew wouldn't be there.

She checked her watch. 7:35 am.

The bus should be here by now, she thought to herself.

Her neighborhood was situated in the quieter area of Redwick, where Saturday mornings were spent sleeping in as there weren't many children running up and down the streets to wake her up. The neighborhood being small, Winter was the only middle schooler who waited for the bus each morning.

Any minute now.

Looking around the corner, she spotted the school bus approaching her stop. "Finally."

"Finally what?" an unfamiliar voice chirped.

Winter turned, startled. In front of her was a young girl about her age, maybe a couple of years younger. She was covered head to toe in freckles, a trait that some people disliked, but Winter adored. Her strawberry-blonde hair rippled in the cool late August breeze, reminding Winter of a long-lost friend.

"I meant the bus. It's finally here."

"Oh, thank God. I thought I'd missed it for sure. It's my first day at middle school, you see. I'm not used to this bus route yet. I tried to be on time, but I overslept."

Winter laughed. "It's okay. It happens to the best of us."

The bus stopped just in front of them. Winter and the girl walked up the steps, their footsteps echoing across the bus as they made their way to the back. When Winter located an empty seat, she gestured for the girl to sit with her.

"That was really nice of you," the girl said. "I just moved here. I don't have any friends here yet."

"That's not true. You've already made a friend. Me."

The girl smiled, extending her hand. "I'm Eleanor."

Winter shook her hand. "I'm Winter. Winter Barnes."

Acknowledgments

I would like to thank the following:

My grandmother, Jane E. Ruth, who sparked my interest in writing in the first place.

My third-grade teacher, Mrs. Smith, whose daily morning assignments helped lay a strong foundation for my editing skills.

My friends in England, for always sticking by my side.

My friends in Virginia, for giving me the confidence to turn my idea into a written story.

My friends in Pennsylvania, for encouraging me when I needed it most.

My parents, who have done nothing but support me in my endeavors.

My brother, for providing a reliable source of jokes and laughter.

My extended family, who never ceased to have faith in me.

Thank you all, truly.

I'm Charlotte Ruth. I wrote this story across two years, finally publishing it at the age of seventeen.

I've always loved to write. *The Whispering* began as a short story idea for NaNoWriMo 2020. I wanted to write a book set in a small town. As a person who has moved around several times, I greatly appreciate the environment of a friendly, tightly-knit small town where everyone knows each other. Thus, I created Redwick.

I look forward to writing many more stories in the future.

CPSIA information can be obtained
at www.ICGtesting.com
Printed in the USA
BVHW030932311022
650735BV00014B/344